THE VEGETABLE MUSEUM

THE VEGETABLE MUSEUM

MICHELLE MULDER

ORCA BOOK PUBLISHERS

Library and Archives Canada Cataloguing in Publication

Mulder, Michelle, 1976–, author
The vegetable museum / Michelle Mulder.

Issued in print and electronic formats.
ISBN 978-1-4598-1679-4 (softcover).—ISBN 978-1-4598-1680-0 (PDF).—
ISBN 978-1-4598-1681-7 (EPUB)

I. Title.

PS8626 U435 V44 2019   jc813'.6   c2018-904890-5
c2018-904891-3

Library of Congress Control Number: 2018954091
Simultaneously published in Canada and the United States in 2019

Summary: In this middle-grade novel, thirteen-year-old Chloë learns about her family's history while helping her grandfather in his garden.

Orca Book Publishers is dedicated to preserving the environment and has printed this book on Forest Stewardship Council® certified paper.

Orca Book Publishers gratefully acknowledges the support for its publishing programs provided by the following agencies: the Government of Canada, the Canada Council for the Arts and the Province of British Columbia through the BC Arts Council and the Book Publishing Tax Credit.

Edited by Tanya Trafford
Cover design by Julie McLaughlin and Rachel Page
Cover artwork by Julie McLaughlin

ORCA BOOK PUBLISHERS
orcabook.com

Printed and bound in Canada.

22 21 20 19 • 4 3 2 1

For my family—past, present and future

ONE

Five rows of red, yellow and green knitting, stitched onto a Stop sign. This is the most interesting thing I've seen since tiptoeing out of our building half an hour ago.

In Montreal right now, the streets are busy with people scraping ice off windshields, shopkeepers calling out good morning to each other, and neighbors shoveling sidewalks. Here in Victoria, though, everyone's still asleep, like they can't stand to face another day of taupe houses, manicured lawns and gray skies.

I touch the matted, damp yarn with one finger. I miss our old neighborhood—the smells of roasting coffee (like burnt toast until you recognize it) and spicy Ethiopian food, flower gardens sprouting in parking lots, murals appearing in alleyways overnight, and little libraries popping up in public parks. Even the yarn bombing was better there. A few months ago, someone knitted an entire rainbow sleeve for a Stop sign. This tiny little yarn tag is nothing compared to that.

Dad says I'll drive myself crazy if I keep comparing where we are to where we were, but I can't help it.

"Fine color choice." It's a man's voice.

I spin around and see my grandfather smiling at me. With half of his mouth anyway. He had a stroke last year, and part of his face is paralyzed.

I don't know him all that well—didn't see him much until we moved in across the street—but he's an unusual guy. His big passion is growing "heirloom vegetables," which as far as I can tell means weird ones that no one else bothers with, like black tomatoes, blue lettuce and purple beans. When he first told me about them, I thought he was losing it. Dad said that some people who have strokes wind up with dementia. So when my grandfather first mentioned the vegetables, I half expected him to add that "Jack and the Beanstalk" is a true story, and fairies live in his compost pile.

"You're out early," I say, as if I'm not totally freaked that he snuck up on me like that. (Not that I'm scared of my own grandfather, of course. But I should have heard him at least. Jeez. One week out of the city, and I've lost all my street smarts.)

"Morning walk," he says. "Never miss it."

"So I heard." He was in rough shape when he first got out of the hospital, but apparently every day he insisted on walking around the block, even if it was pouring rain.

"Your handiwork?" He points to the wisps of yarn.

"Nah, I'd have made it bigger and more colorful." I don't know why I say this, like I'm some kind of closet yarn bomber. I knit, but only socks and sweaters.

"Fair enough. The street could use more color." He surveys the houses, lawns and boulevard. "So which way now? You coming or going?"

I shrug. "I'm heading home, I guess."

He says nothing as we walk. He drags one leg a bit, and I wonder if he has to concentrate to get his body to move. We pass a driveway where a man in a suit is getting into a car. "Morning, Uli."

My grandfather's name is Ulrich, but everyone calls him Uli, even me. Uli waves at the man. We keep walking. At the corner, he glances up at a bare Stop sign. "Another one that could use more color. Orange and yellow maybe. Or a green post with knitted petals around the sign?"

I study his face for a moment and then smile. I don't think he's teasing me. "You're really getting into this."

"Makes people stop and pay attention," he says. "I like unusual."

Like the vegetables. I've discovered since moving here that Uli is way more interesting than I'd imagined. Dad never talked about him much. In all my thirteen years, we never once came to visit. The only thing I remembered about Uli was that he was very tall and got really excited about going to the botanical gardens the time he visited us in Montreal. And we went out for ice cream after. That's it. Every time

I asked Dad about him, he changed the subject. Then Uli had a stroke, and Dad decided the two of us should move here. Without Mom. My parents hadn't been getting along, but I sure didn't see this move coming.

Uli stops in front of his little house. It's the third of three almost identical gray stucco houses with different-colored doors. Uli's is the one on the corner, with the green door. If you drive by quickly, it looks like an ordinary place. But from here on the sidewalk, you can see that the green stuff growing in the front yard isn't grass. It's some other kind of plant, one you don't have to mow. Uli calls it "creeping thyme." He says that in summer, when you step on it, it smells like pizza. (That was another moment when I thought my grandfather might be completely nuts, but Dad told me later that lots of people put thyme in their tomato sauce.) To the right of the front walk is a big tree. It doesn't have any leaves on it yet, but Uli told me it's an apple.

A huge cedar hedge extends out from both sides of the house and frames the backyard. There's a solid wooden gate in the hedge, just behind the apple tree, and through there, in the back, is where Uli grows his vegetables. I haven't gone through that gate yet though—or been into the house either, for that matter, which is a bit weird. Another thing Dad won't explain. Uli says there's nothing to see in his garden right now anyway because it's still winter, but that doesn't make me any less curious. On my way to school, I walk past the sidewalk side of the hedge, and one time I noticed a bit of a hole near the far corner. I pushed a branch aside and stuck my head in, but all I could see was the back of a greenhouse. I didn't dare go farther in, in case someone spotted me.

"Here, let me show you something." Uli points at one of the cherry blossom trees that the city planted between the sidewalk and the road. It's all bark and pink blossoms right now, even though other trees—like the apple in Uli's yard—are still completely bare. The blossoms were the first thing I noticed when we got here last week. I took a picture to send to Mom, because she'd told me about them. She's been to the west coast for conferences at this time of year. She said sometimes whole streets are lined with pink blossoms. If you walk under them, they shower petals on you, and it's called a pink-out because it happens while everyone else in the country is battling winter blizzards and whiteouts.

These trees look different from the ones Mom showed me in pictures though. These ones have two kinds of flowers. Most of them are super frilly, but the blossoms on the lower branches are simpler and a different shade of pink. Uli reaches up and cups a few of the less-frilly flowers in one hand. "Around July, these'll turn into cherries. The dark kind. Delicious."

Huh. I thought Dad said cherry blossom trees were just for show. No fruit. And he should know. He grew up on this street, after all. Again I study my grandfather's face, looking for a hint that he's teasing. If he is, I can't tell. "This is my public artwork," he adds, like he planted the trees himself. Maybe he did, for all I know.

"They're beautiful," I say.

"I don't mean all the blossoms." He waves a hand at the tree. "Just these ones here at the ends.

I grafted on fruit-bearing cherries. Every tree for the next four blocks is fruit-bearing now. The cherries come out right at picking height, perfect for snacking in July."

I follow his gaze down the street. Sure enough, every light-pink tree has different flowers on the lower tips. "Grafting?" I ask. "Isn't that for skin? Like for burn victims?"

He nods. "Yes, but it works for trees too."

"That's actually pretty cool," I say. "Like yarn bombing with live plants."

"Yarn bombing? That's what the knitting on the sign posts is called?" He shakes his head. "Should have a less-violent name. I've lived in bombed-out cities. A burst of color on a drab street is nothing like that."

"You were in a bombing?" I ask.

He puts his hand on my shoulder. "I'll tell you about it sometime. Now you need to get ready for school."

I don't argue. In five minutes, I've already learned more about my grandfather than I ever did from my dad. I give Uli a quick hug. "See you later. Maybe after school?"

When I reach the other sidewalk, he calls my name. I turn to see him moving slowly toward me. I go back to save him a trip.

"This neighborhood might look plain at first," he says, "but I know you'll find its heartbeat. I hope you'll be very happy here."

He talks like this is a permanent move, like we'll be here forever. I don't want to disappoint him, but as far as I can tell, we've only come to Victoria to wait. For any number of things. For Uli to be fine on his own again. Or for Dad to find a better job. Or for him and Mom to want to live together again. Or all, or none, of the above. As soon as we're done waiting, we'll go back to Montreal and continue on with our lives.

I don't want to hurt Uli's feelings though. Instead I think about the cherry blossoms and how getting to know my grandfather might be the only decent thing that comes out of this temporary transplant to this side of the country. "Thanks." I put a hand on his weak arm. He clasps my hand with his good one.

TWO

I know the apartment will be empty when I get back. A few months ago, you'd never have caught Dad awake before eight. (Early mornings are Mom's department. She's out the door by six thirty because, as she says, she does her best thinking before everyone else gets to the university.) Dad used to roll out of bed as late as possible. He could dress, shave, comb his hair and grab a smoothie from the fridge in about ten minutes. When I heard the front door open, I'd run down the hall, grab my backpack and follow him out.

Dad lost his job at Brockhurst in November. He'd been the Social Studies teacher at my school since before I was born, and every day after he left,

I had to listen to kids rehashing the details of him getting sacked. All my life, he'd spent our drives home ranting about young people who were born with silver spoons in their mouths, but he'd always kept his views under wraps at school. Then one day he caught Kaitlin Green showing off her new phone when she was supposed to be working on her Industrial Revolution assignment. He snapped. Kaitlin ran out of the classroom in tears, and a week later Dad was eating ripple chips on the couch.

My best friend—her name's Sofia—and I tried to convince my parents to let me transfer to our neighborhood school. Actually, we'd been trying for ages, because I'd never really fit in at Brockhurst. Everyone else who went there lived in a mansion and had a driver to bring them to campus. I showed up in Dad's twelve-year-old hatchback. Everyone knew we weren't rich enough to really belong, but most of my school fees were covered because Dad worked there. Until he moved to Ripple Chip Land, that is.

In the end, none of Sofia's and my efforts mattered anyway. In January, Dad announced that he'd found a job in Victoria and that I was going out west with him. Mom agreed that it was for the best, since she travels so much for work, and she said she'd come visit me in March. No one asked me what I wanted. When I threatened to disappear just before the plane left, my parents both laughed. Together. As a unit, for once.

I would have thought a job good enough to move across the country for would be a real humdinger, as my grandfather would say. One that came with a big salary, amazing benefits and incredible job satisfaction. But my dad's gone from teaching at one of the most prestigious private schools in Montreal to managing a dumpy apartment building across the street from where my grandfather lives. The Suffolk Arms is as old and hideous as the faux-fancy name suggests.

Our hallway smells like a chain-smoker. So does our apartment. I fumble in the dark for the light switch, and the bare bulb in the hallway flicks on. Except for a few coats and shoes in the closet, our place is mostly empty because we only had a suitcase and two small backpacks when we got here.

Dad didn't want us to bring anything more because he didn't want Mom to feel like we were leaving her. (Uh, hello?) I said we should at least bring the houseplants, on humanitarian grounds—I once found a cactus in Mom's office that died from lack of water—but Dad said we needed a fresh start. So here we are, furnitureless and fresh in a crappy apartment. We each have a mattress now and a few dishes, but that's as far as we've got in the interior-decorating department. Dad has big plans for this place, but as far as I'm concerned, no matter what he does to redecorate, it's still going to be a dumpy place with views of a parking lot.

The door opens behind me. "Up and dressed already!" Dad wipes his forehead on the back of his hand. He's drenched in sweat, but he's got a smile on his face, two things that rarely happen together. My dad's a big man, and he used to be some incredible outdoor endurance athlete when he was a teenager. But in my lifetime, I'd never once seen him intentionally exercise. Until we moved here. "Looks like we're both turning over new leaves."

"I went for a walk," I say.

"Discover anything interesting in the 'hood?"

I don't mention the fruit grafting. Dad hasn't warned me away from my grandfather, but he hasn't exactly encouraged me and Uli to get to know each other either. Even though we've moved across the country because of Uli, Dad is still very particular about our time together. We run errands. We go to restaurants. I haven't been inside my grandfather's house yet, and he hasn't come over here. I'll keep our early-morning conversation to myself for now.

I guess Dad takes my silence for complete disgust with my surroundings. "Give it time, Chloë." He claps me on the shoulder. "It'll get better." Then he tells me how he met one of our neighbors running along the beach this morning. The guy has a friend who's moving and wants to sell his furniture. "By the time you come home from school, I might have this place all decked out!"

He's so excited that I can't help but smile. One happy parent is better than none, right? I keep telling myself that. Maybe by the time we move back to Montreal, I'll believe it.

Apart from Mom, the person I miss most right now is Sofia. We were neighbors in Montreal and have been best friends since I was two. Other families on our street came and went, but ours were permanent fixtures. On schooldays she always showed up on our doorstep about five minutes after Dad and I got home. We did homework together, ate supper at whichever house had the best menu and hung out until bedtime. The first few days after I left, we were texting all the time, but that made me feel even farther away.

This street only has two kids my age. One apparently lives in our building, but he's off visiting relatives, so I haven't met him yet. The other guy lives in the little gray house with the brown door, next to my grandfather's. On my second day here, I noticed him sitting on his front steps, playing with a black rat on a leash. Rats creep me out, but Sofia challenged me to introduce myself to one new person a day. So when I saw the same kid in my math class at school, I got up the nerve to talk to him. "Hi, I'm Chloë. I just moved into the building across from your house."

"I know," he said. I already knew his name was Slater, but he didn't bother to introduce himself. Instead he looked around to make sure other kids were listening. "You guys had the pest-control van come to your place yesterday, right? I hear bedbugs really suck."

A few kids laughed.

"Har, har." I wished my face didn't feel so hot. "It was just a routine check. It's not like the place is infested."

"Uh-huh."

Jerk. I sat down, pretending to ignore the whispers behind me. I could imagine what they were saying—*That new girl? Don't get too close or you'll start scratching too*—and I didn't bother introducing myself to anyone else after that.

But faces are becoming familiar as the weeks go by. Once in a while I smile at some of them. Mostly they smile back. I act as if Slater doesn't exist, which can get tricky because we walk home at the same time every day. (Except Thursdays, when he walks in the opposite direction, with his soccer cleats hanging off his backpack. I love Thursdays.) Today, I am half a block ahead. I can feel his eyes on me.

I step onto the patchy grass in front of our building. To be honest, I don't blame Slater for thinking we have bedbugs—or any number of other pests. A month ago this place was all long grass, flaking paint, burned-out lightbulbs and broken, faded fencing around the back parking lot. Dad's tackled most of it, and the place is looking much better, but even if it was a dump, who is Slater MacIntyre to point that out? He lives with a creature known for carrying the bubonic plague, and his house is no palace either.

I hear a grunt near the front door of our building. A guy my age I've never seen before has two bulging bags of groceries hanging from one arm, and he's wrestling with a key in the lock. His long black ponytail hangs down past the collar of his denim jacket. Flames are embroidered up both arms, and he's wearing sandals, despite the

March rain. He yanks at the key, can't get it out, kicks the door and howls in pain. Eventually he gets the key out of the door, which he props open with one elbow. I think of tiptoeing around to the back entrance, so he won't know I've seen this whole embarrassing scenario, but now he's trying to push a box full of food into the building with his foot. I step forward and hold open the door.

"Whoa. Where'd you come from?" he asks.

"I live here."

"Cool!"

Together we get the box through. He puts his bags down, wipes one hand on his jeans and holds it out to me. I hesitate for a second before I shake. It just seems so formal.

"I'm Nikko," he says. "You must be Chloë. Welcome to the Suffolk-ating Arms!"

I laugh. "Thanks."

"How's Victoria so far? I mean, you moved here from Montreal, right? My mum told me. You've probably seen her around. Japanese woman, tiny glasses?" He makes circles with his thumbs and index fingers and holds them up to his face. "Not that there are a lot of Japanese people around here, with or without glasses. You've probably noticed that by now. This whole neighborhood is white. Not like Vancouver. Or Montreal. Are you liking it okay? Here, I mean? It must be a big change."

The words come nonstop. He's out of breath by the time he finishes talking, and I smile. He's the friendliest person I've met so far. I don't want to hurt his feelings by saying how boring his city is, so I try to think of something positive to say. "I like being this close to the ocean." That's true, at least. I've gone down to the rocky beach almost every day since we got here. That, Uli's stories and my texts to and from Sofia are the only things keeping me sane right now. Dad hasn't said a word about when we're going back to Montreal. Mom hasn't either.

Mom acts as if we're here for good. She calls every two days, tells me about funny things students have said in her classes or about international conferences she's looking into. Yesterday we talked about her trip here next weekend. She's renting a car, and the two of us are driving to Tofino, about six hours away. She says she wants to try the rugged west-coast thing that Dad always raves about, but her version of rugged is a lodge by the beach. Which is fine with me. The place she booked has a TV and a Jacuzzi—much more our style than Dad's. He'd stay on the beach in a tent in the pouring rain.

Nikko looks at me, and I realize I've totally missed what he said. Something about the ocean. Not sure how to respond, I change the topic. "You've been away, right? That's why I haven't seen you around? My dad told me."

"Yup, I was visiting my grandparents. In Revelstoke. That's on the other side of BC, in the mountains. I go every winter."

"Nice. Must be good to get a break from school."

"Nah," he says, "I homeschool. I can log on from wherever, and believe me, my grandparents make sure I do. They've never quite understood the whole homeschool thing. At first they thought I was going to wind up completely illiterate and anti-social. They've chilled out a bit now, but they're strict about how many hours I study a day."

"Huh." Homeschooling explains his outfit. He'd never last a day at school with Slater.

"Your dad's doing a great job." Nikko nods at the lobby walls. Dad painted them last week. He cleaned the carpets too, and this week he plans to put in better lighting. Somehow he still finds time to go hiking or kayaking every day. He'd never kayaked in his life before we got here, but within days of arriving he'd signed up for lessons and joined a club that rents out boats. Go figure. It's like all those weeks on the couch at home, he was storing up energy that burst out when we got to the west coast. He keeps threatening to take me out on these outdoor adventures too. In the summer, he says, we can swim in something called the Gorge. He swears it's cleaner than any of the nearby lakes. But what's wrong with a proper indoor pool, I'd like to know?

"The last caretaker was a bit of a disaster," Nikko says.

"No kidding."

"Estelle on the third floor got on his case all the time. She's the capital *S* in Suffolk-ating Arms, by the way. Have you met—?"

"Yes." I interrupt because it seems like the only way to make him pause for breath. "She showed up on our first day with a list of stuff for Dad to do. She called every day until it was done."

Nikko tells me about some of the other neighbors, an old guy on the fourth floor who's the building's friendliest, a lady on the second who is some kind of fortune-teller, and Estelle's cat, who watches everything that goes on in the parking lot when Estelle can't be there to do it herself. Soon Nikko's talking about the cars and how he can tell who's coming and going by the sound of each engine. "Our family doesn't have a car though. We bike everywhere. Mostly, anyway. We're part of a car share too, but mostly we bike. We should go together sometime. On a bike ride, I mean. I'll show you around. Maybe you've already been exploring, but I could show you some places you might not have discovered yet."

The thought of me on a bicycle makes me almost laugh out loud. Sofia has been bugging me to learn to ride for years, but I never saw the point. Everything I wanted to do was within walking distance. "No bike. Sorry," I say, although I'm really not.

Nikko looks at me, wide-eyed. "You can't live in Victoria without a bike. You're missing too much! I'll find one for you, and then I'll show you the city." The elevator doors open. He places the box of food on one hip, hoists up the bags and hobbles into the elevator. "I'll let you know when I find you some wheels."

The doors close. I shake my head, but I'm smiling as I pull out my phone. I haven't texted Sofia since yesterday, when I sent her a selfie of me standing on the rocky beach.

Greetings from the west coast. Note the lack of sports gear.

From the moment I'd told Sofia that I was going west, she'd teased me about becoming a granola-eating yogi who went everywhere by bike and dressed like a hiker for every occasion. She said that's what happens when people move out here. I'd laughed it off, but it still felt important to point out that the same old me could enjoy the beach without becoming someone else entirely.

I'm sure Sofia was laughing when she answered my text.

Matter of time. Happy metamorphosis!

Now, on my way down the hall, I tell her about Nikko.

Met the other kid in our building. Wants to know if I have a bike.

Her answer is instantaneous.

Congrats, my beautiful butterfly!

Flap. Flap. Flap.

THREE

"Hi, Chloë-bear." Mom sounds tired. It's eleven o'clock in Montreal. I wonder if she's just getting home from work.

"What's up, Mom?" I cradle my phone on my shoulder so I can keep knitting. I've almost finished the pair of socks I started when we got here. Turquoise and purple with a Turkish heel. Mom's size.

"Honey, things are turning out differently than I expected."

She's probably trying to tell me she has to bring work to Tofino this weekend. As if this is big news. She always works part of the weekend. The most important thing is that she'll be here, on this side of the country. She booked the lodge the day Dad bought our flights to Victoria. She stuck the reservation printouts in my How-to-Survive-This-Move kit, along with a homemade calendar so I could count down the days. She promised we'd spend every second catching up, but I'm fine with a few hours on my own. It's not the end of the world.

"I have to resubmit a major piece of research by Tuesday." Her voice is tight.

"Don't worry about it, Mom. You're flying across the country to see me. I'm not going to be offended if you have to work a bit while you're here."

Silence stretches between us, and my stomach twists. "You're still coming, aren't you? I mean, you've already got a ticket and—"

"I'm sorry, Chloë. You know how much I was looking forward…"

I feel like hurling the phone across the room.

Mom's babbling on about how she'll make it up to me when I press *End*. I'm moving in slow motion. If I move any faster, I might explode. I pick up her homemade calendar with its cute drawings, and I shred it in two, then four. The pieces flutter to the bottom of my wastebasket.

Next I consider my closed door. I need to get out. Now. But on the other side, Dad is cooking supper. One look at me and he'll know what's happened. If he sees me now and he tries to help, I'll fall apart completely.

I climb out the window and head for the beach. Easy escape. Our crappy first-floor apartment has something going for it after all.

"Here we go." I set our plates on the table and slide into a chair next to Dad.

"Thanks for supper." Uli picks up his burrito. It's Tuesday evening, which means we eat at a restaurant and do the grocery shopping afterward. On Thursdays, we all go for a walk together, same time every week, same route down to the ocean and back. Dad calls Uli daily but doses out visits like medication, measured to the minute.

Tonight's restaurant is a Mexican one downtown, hidden away in the middle of a mall. I don't know how Dad finds these places.

We always ate at home in Montreal. "Why pay top dollar for something you could make yourself?" he'd ask if I mentioned a new Afghan place on the corner or the Sri Lankan one down the street. Then he'd go online. A few days later he'd present his homemade traditional Afghan *mantu* (meat dumplings) or Sri Lankan green jackfruit curry. Not that I'm complaining. I love his cooking. But it's strange that now, after we have moved to Dullsville, he's so into eating out.

"Weather's warming up," says Uli. "Planting time. Should have had the soil ready by now."

Dad gives him a sharp look. "You're not planning on gardening, are you? That's way too much bending and lifting for you."

"Where there's a will, there's a way," Uli says.

"I've heard that before."

I look back and forth between them. They glare at each other.

"I made a promise," Uli says, "to the people who gave me the seeds. Darned if I'll go back on it now."

Dad takes a deep breath, lifts his burrito and starts eating like he's the only one at the table. I feel sorry for Uli. The whole vegetable thing reminds me of when Sofia visited her great-aunt last summer, and the old woman wanted help sorting her plastic-bag collection. What do you say to a super-old person with who knows how much longer to live who wants nothing more than to sort plastic bags (or grow vegetables that no one wants)? How do you tell them they're wasting their precious time?

The silence is getting awkward. Someone needs to say something. It looks like it'll have to be me. I turn to Uli. "Where did you get the seeds for your vegetables anyway?"

"I've got a list of people as long as your arm. The first old fellow, I met at a retirement home I gardened for. He'd come sit on a bench while I planted flowers or pruned the trees. One day he gives me a small envelope. Purple beans, he says. His great-great-great-grandmother grew them back in Italy, and his mother smuggled them over here when they moved to Canada. He grew them himself for years but didn't have anywhere to plant them anymore. He wanted to know if I'd grow them. To keep the line going."

"The line?" I ask.

"Line of seeds," he says. "Let 'em sit around too long, and they lose their growing power. Get too lackadaisical with this kind of thing, and the only string beans left on the planet will be the flavorless supermarket kind. Blech. Wait till you try the varieties people used to eat. The flavor will knock your socks off."

It's hard to imagine getting that excited about beans, but who knows? Maybe they'll surprise me. "If they're so great, why don't the stores carry them?"

"They don't keep as well," Uli says. "If you grow them yourself, that doesn't matter. You just pick them when you need them. The thing is to grow them every year, though, and save the seeds for the next season."

"Or give them to someone who believes in endangered vegetables."

"Bingo. I've got more seeds and stories than you can shake a stick at now. Pink broccoli from Russia. Blue kale from Scotland."

"All smuggled?" I ask.

"Probably, but decades and decades ago. Families grew them here for generations before I got them. I wouldn't have taken them otherwise. Seeds from far away are too risky. They might have diseases that could wipe out a whole garden."

"Huh." I had to admit this was more interesting than I'd imagined—family heirlooms you can keep growing generation after generation. Who knew our family even had any keepsakes to pass down?

I glance at my dad. His face has relaxed again. Maybe Uli's noticed that too, because he makes another attempt at conversation. "Muriel brought me the paper today." His home-care nurse is always doing thoughtful things like that. Much as Uli hated the idea of someone coming around to the house every day, I think he enjoys her visits now. "Saved it for you, in case you want to read it."

"Thanks," Dad says. "Anything interesting?"

"Only read the gardening section. It was all about flowers though."

"Flowers aren't your thing?" I ask.

He shakes his head and gives me his strange half smile. "I'd rather read about pre-Civil War peanuts, or fish peppers, but no such luck. There was an interesting article on earthworms though. Did you know the worms in an acre of soil can till eighteen tons of dirt each year?"

I picture an army of worms with little hoes and cowboy hats on. You've got to admire a guy who gets excited about something so simple. It reminds me of Sofia's little brother, Jordan, who's three and does a happy dance every time he finds a bug in their garden.

I take another bite of burrito. It's better than I expected. Uli keeps talking, telling us how Charles Darwin spent years proving that earthworms make conscious decisions about how to pull leaves and pine needles into their burrows. "He wrote a whole book about it."

"I bet that was a bestseller."

"You bet your bootstraps, young lady!"

I laugh, and Uli keeps feeding us earthworm trivia. When that runs out, we all focus on our food. We're the only quiet table in the whole restaurant. I can't help thinking about Mom, probably in her office, hunched over her computer. When I told Dad she had bailed on Tofino, he was furious. That same night, he booked two tickets to Montreal. We go home in ninety-nine days. He booked return flights too, but I didn't dare point out that there's no way I'm coming back here with him. I'll deal with that later. Meanwhile, we've both agreed not to talk about Mom right now.

"Excuse me. Nature calls." Dad stands up to go to the bathroom, leaving me alone with my grandfather. I seize the opportunity.

"Hey, Uli. Remember a few weeks ago, when you talked about the bombed-out cities? You promised you'd tell me about it sometime."

He takes a deep breath and glances after my dad. "You know where I was born, I guess."

"Germany," I say. During the Second World War. I think that's what Dad said.

Uli shakes his head. "Poland. My family was German though. Russians invaded, and my mother and I escaped with the clothes on our backs."

And somehow Dad never thought to mention this to me?

"I was three," Uli continues, "so I don't remember that part, but we stayed with relatives in East Germany for a while before crossing to West Germany. That part I do remember, running in the dark with bullets flying. We slept wherever we could—in barns, sometimes in bombed-out churches."

My burrito has turned to stone in my stomach. It's one thing to read about the war in a textbook, another to hear about your grandfather sleeping in a bomb crater.

Dad returns, wiping his hands on his jeans. "Ridiculous. The bathroom's at the end of the earth, you need a key, which is back here, and they're out of paper towels—hey, are you two okay?" He looks back and forth between us.

I realize I have tears in my eyes. "Uli was telling me about escaping from Poland when he was a kid."

I expect Dad to nod solemnly and look concerned—these must be painful memories for Uli—but his sigh sounds exasperated.

Uli holds up a hand. "Don't worry, Darryl. I'll stop."

"Why?" I ask.

"Your father's heard this story a million times, Chloë."

"But I haven't," I say. "And it's part of my history too, right?"

Uli looks at Dad like he's asking if it's okay to keep talking.

"Go ahead. Whatever," says my dad. He takes another bite of his burrito. "Great. Now it's cold. I'm going to ask them to reheat it."

"What's up with him?" I ask Uli as Dad gets to his feet again.

"I talked a lot about Europe when he was a kid. I thought he should know where he came from. Maybe I overdid it."

I bite my lip. "Is that why things are so tense between you?" I blurt out. "I mean, why you never visited each other? Why you hardly ever came to Montreal?"

Uli's hands fall to his lap, and his right eye is wet. He sniffs and shakes his head. "You'll have to ask your dad about that, Chloë. I can tell you more about Europe though." He talks quickly. "Mother knew we had cousins in Germany. We never did find them, but she also had a sister in Canada. Mother remembered the address, so she thought we'd head here. She worked three jobs to pay for the tickets."

"Where was your dad in all this?" I ask.

"The Russians shot him. I was a toddler," Uli says with no emotion whatsoever. "I don't remember him at all."

Dad sits down again, his burrito steaming. Uli glances at him. "Don't worry. I'll keep it short." He describes the little town on the Baltic Sea where he and his mom lived. "She died when I was ten though."

"What?" Another crucial detail Dad's never mentioned. "How did she die?"

"I don't know," Uli says. "She didn't want to spend money on a doctor. She just got thinner and thinner, and—"

Dad brushes off his fingers. "Are you two finished eating? I'll take the plates up to the counter."

"Thanks," Uli says while I watch my father get up yet again. I can't believe he'd butt in when Uli's talking about his mother dying. But Uli carries on as if nothing happened. "Some neighbors took me in. They gave me a choice: I could stay with them, or they could help me get to Canada to be with my aunt."

Dad comes back and stands by the table until we both get up and put on our coats. He helps Uli with his.

"I chose Canada, obviously. That's what my mother had wanted."

"What was your aunt like?" I ask.

Dad rolls his eyes. Uli squeezes my shoulder. "Let's leave that story for another time, Chloë. I've tortured your father enough for one evening."

In the car, conversation drifts back to safe topics like earthworms and the national budget. Dad drives us across town to the huge grocery store, and we buy our supplies. By the time we're back outside, it's pouring rain. We get drenched on our way across the parking lot.

"Tell me again why we can't just buy food a block from home?" I ask. Every week since we got here, we've driven halfway across the city to get groceries, even though Smith's store is just down the street. It can't possibly be worse than some of the little places we shopped at in Montreal. Sure, it always looks kind of dark inside, but plenty of people go in and out all the time. None of them ever have the horrified look Dad gets on his face when I mention it.

My shopping question was designed to bug him, to get him to show some feeling about something. I'm still mad about how he treated Uli at the restaurant. I asked my grandfather to tell that story, and Dad acted like Uli was some old guy who talked too much.

"Wouldn't catch me dead in that place." Uli spits on the ground next to him, like I've fed him poison.

I must look stunned, because Dad gives me a sympathetic look. "It's a long story, Chloë."

I can tell there's no point in asking more questions. We're all silent as we climb into the car. Back at Uli's, Dad and I carry his bags of food up his front steps and leave them at the top. I hug my grandfather good night, and we leave before he opens his front door.

"So what's the deal between you two?" I ask Dad when we're back at our place. I've never gotten anywhere with this question before—*I'll tell you when you're older*, he always says—but maybe after his performance tonight as The Heartless Son, he'll be embarrassed enough to cough up some explanations.

Dad pulls a box of crackers from a bag and shoves it into a cupboard. "My father had a terrible childhood. I understand why hearing about it affects you so much. But I grew up hearing it used as an excuse for every screwup. It got old pretty quick."

"What screwups?" I ask.

"Look, Chloë," Dad says. "Let's leave the past in the past, where it belongs."

I can't believe he's brushing me off again. "You're telling *me* that? You hardly talked to him for decades. Now you can barely stand to be in the same room with him, and you're telling *me* to leave the past in the past?"

My dad yanks a hunk of cheese from a bag and slams it onto the counter. "Chloë, this is not a conversation I'm prepared to have right now. We came here because I need to lay some things to rest with my father. But it's hard for me, okay? I don't want to make it hard for you, too, by telling you the whole story. Your mother's given you enough to deal with."

That kind of makes sense. I tone it down a bit. "Just tell me a few basic things, okay? I mean, he's safe to be with, right? He's not an ax murderer or anything?"

Dad sighs, leans his elbows on the counter and puts his head in his hands. When he looks up, his eyes are red. "No, he's not an ax murderer, Chloë.

And in some ways he was a very good father. But we have some stuff to work through, that's all." His eyes meet mine, and they're not hard like they were at the restaurant. They look sad, like he can't bear to have this conversation. And the pain in his eyes scares me. So I drop the topic.

For now anyway.

FOUR

"Maybe your grandfather wouldn't let your dad marry his high-school sweetheart," Sofia says when she calls the next day. "Your dad was so mad that he didn't talk to his father for years. Then, this winter, when he realized Uli wasn't long for this world, he decided it was time to resolve past issues."

No matter how messed-up life gets, I can always rely on Sofia to make me laugh. "Trust you to turn family politics into a sappy romance novel."

"I'm just saying anything could have sparked their fight. They didn't deal with it, and they got angrier as time went by. Remember the Blue Sweatshirt Incident?"

I sigh. "We were six, Sof. And I'm sure my grandfather never accused my dad of stealing a Dora the Explorer top. Besides, it only took a week for us to make up, not twenty-five years."

"But it was the longest week of my life," she says. "By the time my aunt found my sweater in her car, I already had seven pieces of proof that you'd stolen it."

"Seriously?"

Silence. "I never told you? Anyway, I was wrong, okay? I apologized. Several times."

"Yeah, but you never told me about the seven pieces of proof," I tease. "Good grief. It's a wonder you didn't call the police."

"I'd punch you in the shoulder right now, if you were here."

"I love you too," I say. "If you were here, we'd solve the Mystery of the Enraged Family Members together."

"Keep me posted on how it goes."

"You know I will."

I'm halfway through my English homework when I hear the buzzer and dash into the living room. Dad's already answered the ancient intercom though. "Yes, she's here," he says to the box. "Do you want to come in, or should I send her out?"

"Who is it?" I ask.

"Your grandfather." He nods and disappears into the kitchen, leaving me to answer the door.

"Chloë! Just who I wanted to see!" Uli lifts his good arm to put around me, and I hug him, too stunned to speak. He has never come to our apartment before.

I take his elbow and lead him into the living room. With the secondhand lamps and furniture that Dad scored, it looks a whole lot better than it used to. The walls are now a trendy Montreal-coffee-shop orange. I like it. "Did you guys declare a truce or something?" I ask Uli.

"I'm not here to see your dad, actually." He lowers himself onto our couch. "I asked him if I could come over, and he said yes. I have a question for you."

I sit down beside him. "Shoot."

"Would you help me with my garden, please? Weeding and planting seeds?"

"For weird vegetables?" The words fly out of my mouth before I can stop them. Fortunately, my grandfather laughs.

"The heirlooms, yes."

I glance over to the kitchen, but Dad's off in an invisible corner, whistling a song I recognize from his Best of the Nineties playlist. I'm on my own. I really do want to help my grandfather, even if only to hear more stories without having to worry about Dad glaring and sighing through every one. Still, Uli should know what he's getting into if I help him. "I don't have much of a green thumb," I admit. "I grew a bean plant once, but that's it. Our place in Montreal doesn't even have a garden, just a tiny patch of dirt by the front steps. Dad grows sunflowers there."

"Doesn't matter," Uli says. "You'll learn."

"But I might, you know, pull out the wrong plants or something."

"I'll keep an eye on you. You provide the muscle. I'll provide the know-how."

Dad's still whistling. Loud. He's into another song now. This one I don't recognize.

"I'm not all that strong." I lift one skinny arm.

Uli grabs his droopy one and holds it up. "Better than what I've got."

I have no more arguments left. "When do I start?"

He beams at me, like I've just given him a winning lottery ticket. I love that it's so simple to make him happy, and I wonder again what my father's held against him for so many years. With any luck, I'll soon find out. Hopefully, not too many plants will die in the process.

"What about right now?" he asks. "No time like the present."

"This tree's grandmother"—Uli points to the bare-branched one in his front yard—"grew behind the house where I was born."

How is that possible? I picture my great-grand-mother, escaping the Russians with a toddler in one arm and a potted tree in the other. "Didn't you escape with only the clothes on your backs?"

"Mother had an apple in her coat pocket," Uli says. "She told me the story all the time when I was growing up. After my dad was killed, she woke me up early one September morning, before sunrise. She told me we were going on a trip. I started to cry because I wanted to play on the swing in the apple tree behind the house, so she picked an apple and made a promise. When we got to where we were going, she said, she'd plant another tree and build another swing. That calmed me down. We set out, and we ate the apple eventually—small and sour, but we were so hungry it didn't matter. She kept the seeds. Every few days she'd take them out. We'd talk about the beautiful country called Canada where we'd plant our tree."

I'm quiet for a moment. "She never made it."

He shakes his head. "I brought the seeds with me though. I planted them way in the back of my aunt's property, where no one would notice a few extra trees."

"So what was your aunt like anyway?" I ask. "Now that Dad's not here, can you finish the story?"

"She was crazy," Uli says. "She said she heard voices, saw foxes in the living room, you name it. Her husband was a boozer, and his farm was going down the tube. That's why he sponsored me to come over. He needed someone to work the farm. I was a city kid by then though. No use to him. He flew off the handle a lot when he was drinking. One time he got so mad he broke my arm. That's when I left, hitchhiked to Edmonton to seek my fortune."

"You should write a book," I say.

"Nah. Too much work. I'd rather be planting seeds." He shuffles down the garden path toward the gate in the hedge. "Come see the garden."

"Wait." I'm still standing under the tree. "You didn't tell me how this tree got here."

He smiles. "You're a stubborn one, Chloë. That'll stand you in good stead. But that's enough ancient history for one day. I have to go in to take my pills soon. After that I won't have energy to come back out again."

I stay right where I am, under the tree, and refuse to move until I hear the rest of the story. No one else tells me this kind of stuff. Dad's mom died when he was a kid. My mom's parents both kicked it before I was born. My uncle Leo lives in Shanghai. I have no cousins (which Sofia thinks is hilarious because she has dozens—enough for both of us, she says). I never thought much about the whole extended-family thing until I had to leave behind my life in Montreal to get to know one of my only living relatives. The least Uli can do is finish the stories he starts. "Please, Uli? How long would it take to tell me? Thirty seconds? A minute and a half, max?"

Uli sighs and mumbles about a chip off the old block, but he gets on with the story. "When I… moved into this house, I took a trip back to my uncle's farm. I told the new owners my story. They let me take what I needed. That's how this tree got here. Now enough lollygagging. Let's go."

I feel like he hasn't told me the whole story, but at least he answered my question. Maybe I can get more out of him when we're digging in the dirt. He holds open the gate for me.

"Thank you," I say.

"Thank *you*." Who knows if we're talking about the garden, the story or something else entirely?

I hold my breath as I walk through the gateway into this place that I've been hearing about for weeks.

Whatever I've been expecting, this isn't it. It looks like a recycling depot spat up over rows and rows of leaf-covered dirt, with empty plastic bottles sticking up at regular intervals. At the back, near the greenhouse, a few tall plants with crinkly, purplish leaves stand tall.

Uli puts a hand on my shoulder. "Not much to look at now, but come summer, you'll be harvesting more vegetables than you can fit in your fridge." My face must tell him exactly what I think about that idea, because he bursts out laughing. "Quite the enticement for a young person, I know. I tried to bribe your father with brussels sprouts when he was a kid too. That didn't work either."

"It explains a lot though."

"Still doesn't like 'em?"

"Hates 'em."

"And you?"

"Not a fan." But we both know I'm not in this for the veggies. I'm doing this for my grandfather. And maybe for my great-grandmother, who I'm already imagining as some sort of tree spirit flitting around this yard, watching us and celebrating our work. My great-grandmother who desperately wanted to raise her little boy in a peaceful place and never even got to see him grow up.

I have a whole new respect for that apple tree. I wonder if I'll feel something—some sort of DNA memory—when I bite into one of its tiny, sour apples. I look out over the leaves and empty pop bottles, picturing a whole garden of heirloom vegetables that all mean something to someone somewhere, even if they look weird to me.

"That's chickweed," Uli says, pointing to a big patch of tiny plants poking out of the earth.

"Who gave you that one?" I ask.

Uli smiles. "It came on its own. It's a weed, but an edible one. Go collect some. We'll put it in a salad."

"You're kidding, right?"

"Nope. Here." He points to the little plants and holds out his hand until I bend down and pick some for him. He pops the tiny leaves into his mouth. "Go on. Try it."

I do, rubbing off the dirt with my fingers first. "Hmmm. It's actually not bad. For a cross between grass and spinach, I mean." I'm not likely to ever eat it again, but I can tell that my response has made Uli happy. "How much do you want?"

"Oh, a few good handfuls. I'll find something to put it in." He waves me toward the greenhouse.

I follow. "What's with all the plastic bottles?"

"It's my irrigation system," he says. I think he's joking until he explains that each bottle is covered in pinholes. In summer, he fills the bottles every few days with water from the rain barrel. They leak out as much water as the plants need to stay healthy. "Best system money can buy, except I built it for free."

He pulls open the door of the greenhouse and leads me inside. Benches loaded with planting supplies line the walls, and there's a big table in the middle. On top is a faded brown shoebox, its corners worn. He places one hand on the lid and looks at me. "This is it. In here are the seeds for everything we'll grow this year. All the stories too."

He opens the box and pulls out one of what looks like dozens of white envelopes. Inside is a paper packet of seeds, a folded piece of paper and a photo of a plant. It looks like a grapevine, with tiny watermelons hanging down where bunches of grapes would be. "This one is cucamelon," he says. "From Mexico. The waitress at my favorite diner gave me the seeds ages ago. I make pickles every year. I probably still have a jar, if you want to try them."

He pulls out envelope after envelope, showing me pictures of purple leeks, black radishes and a bumpy light-brown bulb called celeriac. The folded pieces of paper tell the story of each seed. I read a few. Each one is like a mini travelogue, tracking where the vegetables came from, who gave Uli the seeds and when. Some even have little world maps at the bottom of the page, tracing the veggie's journey.

"Better get a move on," he says, closing the box. "Let me grab some tools and something for that chickweed."

As he rummages in a corner, I look through the glass of the greenhouse out into the garden.

I imagine the empty rows crowded, as Uli promised, with plant life and vegetables whose ancestors traveled here from all over the world. Uli says that some of them don't even exist in their original countries anymore. The ones we'll grow are the last of their kind. This is nothing like Sofia's great-aunt's plastic-bag collection after all. These are endangered species. And food. And history. And what my grandfather lives for, all wrapped up in one.

FIVE

"Ta-da!"

Nikko and I are standing in our building's parking lot. A few minutes ago he banged on my door (wearing plaid shorts and a Hawaiian shirt, but who am I to judge?) and told me to follow him outside. At first I thought he needed help with another load of groceries. But now I'm staring at a red-and-white bicycle with high handle-bars, a wicker basket and a bell on the front. Sofia would absolutely love this bike. I'm not kidding. It's completely hipster cool and would fit in perfectly in Montreal. I can already picture myself pedaling along the Lachine Canal, my hair flowing out behind me, with a baguette, some cheese and a picnic blanket in my basket.

"Hop on!" Nikko says. "Try it out. I brought a wrench to adjust the seat height."

"I…uh…"

His face falls. "You don't like it? Is it the seat? Mom's got a cushier one in our storage locker." He fumbles in his pocket for keys.

"No! It's not the seat." I feel my face get hot. I'm embarrassed to tell him why, but I don't want him to think I'm ungrateful either. "It's the whole bike… and the fact that I don't know how to ride one." Why didn't I learn when I was six, like every other kid?

"Oh, is that all?" Nikko slips the keys back into his pocket. "I can teach you."

I revise my picture to me pedaling up and down the sidewalk of our apartment building with all the nosy neighbors gawking out their windows. The sight of me wobbling and splatting onto the pavement might even bring a smile to Estelle's face. I open my mouth to tell Nikko that I'm not the sporty type, but then I stop and take a breath. "I…want to ride this bike, but I'd rather skip over the learning part. You know, the bit where I fall off and look like a complete idiot? I could do without that."

"But the fall only lasts a few seconds," he says, and I wonder what it must be like to not care at all what anyone else thinks. "You get back on, keep practicing and get around on your own steam for the rest of your life. So what if you tumble the first few times?"

I glance up at the windows. Estelle's nosy cat is watching us. I picture it snickering.

"We don't have to practice here," Nikko adds. "We can go to the elementary school. That's where I learned to ride. In the parking lot."

When he was, like, four, probably. He waggles his eyebrows at me and looks so ridiculous that I can't help laughing. "Okay. School parking lot it is."

"Great! Meet me back here at four thirty." He's gone before I can ask him what to do with the bike. In the end, I wheel it into our apartment and text a photo to Sofia. She texts back.

Wheeeeeeee! Can he find one for me when I come visit?

I keep telling her that I'm not going to be here long enough for her to visit. Ninety days until I get home, and once I'm there, I'm not leaving.

Flash forward to me sitting on the bicycle behind Sir James Douglas Elementary. The seat is as low as it can go, and Nikko has taken off the pedals. After about ten minutes of arguing, he's also dressed me up in a set of gardening kneepads (borrowed from my grandfather) and sport socks tied around my elbows. He won me over by promising that no one I know will see me now, but people will definitely notice if I go home covered in scrapes and bruises. The crowning glory of my stellar outfit is the large pink helmet, on loan from his mother. I take a deep breath and picture myself pedaling the Lachine Canal, kneepadless, sockless and pink-helmet-free.

"Now sit back, push off with your feet and glide. You're not going to fall, so don't worry about looking like an idiot."

"Idiot? Why would I look like an idiot?" I wave my socked elbows at him.

"Oh, I wish I had a camera! Tomorrow I'll bring one, and you can send the photos to your friends in Montreal. You have Instagram, don't you?" He lifts an imaginary camera to his face. "Smile pretty now!"

"No!" I yell like a crazed bicycle warrior and push off. It doesn't take me long to get the hang of balancing. Soon I'm chasing him around the parking lot, laughing harder than I have in ages.

When I veer past him and glide to a stop, I'm out of breath but grinning. Nikko puts the pedals back on and holds the back of my bike as I wobble to a start. Now comes the hard part. "If you let go, I'll never forgive you!" I shout as he runs behind me. I teeter around the empty parking lot a few times and eventually come to a stop. "I didn't fall!"

"Of course not," he says. "That'll be tomorrow, when I let go. Or the next day." He pulls a watch out of his pocket. (A watch! Who uses watches these days?) "I'd better get home for supper."

"Don't you have a cell phone?"

"Nope. My parents are afraid it'll fry my brain. Radiation and all that."

He rides a bike in traffic every day, and his parents are worried about cell-phone radiation? I show him my phone, so ancient that it would never be mistaken for smart. "Technology addiction is my dad's pet peeve. He's cool about most stuff, but when it comes to technology, even a phone could turn me into a techno-monster."

Nikko sighs. "Parents."

"What are yours like?"

He reaches up and tightens his ponytail. "They both teach yoga. Mom's writing a cookbook. Dad's a musician. He plays the double bass."

I knew that, actually. I've seen his dad load the gigantic instrument onto his bike trailer. Who knew anyone could pull an instrument of that size with a bicycle? Nikko's obviously not the only eccentric in his family. "But what are they like? Strict or chill?"

"Chill, I guess, as long as I follow the rules." He looks at his watch again. "And one of those rules is that I have to be home for supper by six o'clock. Shall we head?"

I take off my mismatched gear, load it into the basket and push my bike toward the sidewalk. "Thanks for the lesson."

"Same time tomorrow?" he asks.

"You sure? It must be boring for you."

He shakes his head. "Anyway, I'll have you riding on the road by the end of the week."

"Drivers of Victoria, watch out."

He smiles, and I blurt out the question that's been bugging me all afternoon. "So, why are you doing this? I mean, getting me a bike and teaching me to ride?"

"Why not? We live in the same building. All my other friends live too far away to ride with."

So basically, I'm better than nothing. Oh well. Beggars can't be choosers, as my grandfather would say.

I fish my phone out of my pocket and pose by my bike. "Do you want to be in my selfie? I'm sending it to a friend in Montreal."

"Hi, honey!" It's nearly nine, almost midnight in Montreal, but Mom is so hyper she sounds like she's downed three enormous lattés. Probably from the

24/7 coffee shop on the corner. I miss that place. Sofia and I used to buy *pains au chocolat* and eat them by the pond in Parc La Fontaine. She says they've changed their supplier and the pastries aren't as good anymore, but I'd still give anything to be sloshing along slushy sidewalks and eating warm pastries with her right now.

"How was your day?" Mom asks. I rest my head on my desk. I'm only halfway through my math homework, I still have a history paper to start, and I don't have the energy to pretend life is wonderful. Dad holed himself up in his room half an hour ago. Tonight he took Uli and me out for cabbage rolls and borscht. Uli started talking about how supermarket food is laced with poisons and has lost all its vitamins by the time it hits our plates. Dad asked if we could just enjoy our meal for once without analyzing it, and Uli shut down. I tried to get conversation going again, but no luck. When I asked Dad later why we moved here if he won't try to get along with his father, he got mad, stalked down the hall, slammed his bedroom door and started lifting weights. Every now and then, I hear a grunt.

"Fine, Mom. Everything's fine."

"Great!" she chirps. "I wanted to let you know I met the deadline."

"Great," I say with zero enthusiasm. I haven't heard from her since she bailed on our weekend in Tofino. Part of me hoped her silence was because she felt awful for being such a crappy parent, but it sounds like she was too busy even for that.

"Chloë, I know you were disappointed. We were both looking forward to time together. I'm sorry it didn't work out."

"It didn't work out because you didn't make it work out." I've been practicing these words since she ditched me.

Mom takes a sharp breath in. "Chloë, I didn't call to argue with you. I wanted to say thank you for giving me the extra time for my deadline."

Unbelievable. "I didn't give you that time. You took it. It's not the same."

"Look, Chloë." The glittering sequins have all fallen away from her voice. "I know the changes of the past few months have been hard on you. But we're doing the best we can, okay?"

"Yeah, well, it still sucks."

"I love you, Chloë," she says. "You know that, right?"

"Yeah."

"And this will all work out. Your father and I are both exactly where we need to be right now. You have to believe that."

"But what about me?"

"You're in the right place too. You're getting to know your grandfather, and you're with your father, who loves you just as much as I do."

I don't say anything. What is there to say?

"Chloë?"

I still don't answer.

"If you're not in the mood for a conversation, we can talk another time. I'm fine with that."

I mumble goodnight, hang up and stare at my math homework. It might as well be in Swahili. I squeeze my eyes shut, wishing everything could be different when I open them again.

SIX

The greenhouse is getting crowded. Uli and I have grown enough tomatoes to keep the whole neighborhood in spaghetti sauce this winter. He planted the seeds in his kitchen a few weeks ago, and the other day he showed me how to transplant them into bigger pots. "Mark Weiss's grandmother smuggled the seeds from Germany," Uli said. "She sewed them into her hat band. The fellows at the border never noticed. Good thing too. These are the best tomatoes I've ever eaten." In a few months, he says, this greenhouse will be like a jungle with big red fruits hanging everywhere. (Yup, tomatoes are fruits because they have seeds. Who knew?)

Out in the garden, tiny pea shoots are poking up. I put a bamboo stick next to each one to give the little sprouts somewhere to climb. In the next row over, I planted hard, wrinkled little fava beans, but first I had to pop each one into my mouth and get it all wet. Apparently, something in our spit—enzymes, Uli says—helps break down the bean's outer coating so it's easier for the sprout to break through. That's what his friend's Turkish grand-mother told him anyway, so he always does that when he plants favas. If spit has anything to do with the towering plant and superlong bean pods in his photo of last year's garden, I'd say it's worth the extra step.

The next row is purple orach, or mountain spinach. (I didn't have to stick those seeds in my mouth, thank goodness. They're so small and papery, they would all stick in my teeth.) Scottish blue kale is the next row after that. We put the tiny cabbage plants in the last row before the hedge. Uli started growing those indoors a few weeks ago too, and for the past few days, he's had to ferry them back and forth between his living room and the front step to harden them off. (That's gardener-speak for "get them used to the cold.") Twelve plants. Three different varieties.

"Who eats this much cabbage?" I ask as I plant. On the stool next to me, Uli lights up as if I'd mentioned chocolate.

"Wait till you try sauerkraut," he says. "I grew up eating it the German way, with caraway seeds and wine in it. But I like the Turkish way even better—with lemon and ginger. Or we could make *rotkraut*—red cabbage cooked with apples. Or roasted cabbage. So many ways to eat it. Just you wait."

I don't have the heart to tell him that in eighty-five days, I'm out of here. But now that I've spent so much time working in the garden, I kind of wish I could see it in its full mad-vegetable glory. I guess Uli can send me pictures. Or maybe Nikko. I'll ask him to help Uli once I'm gone. The harvest is going to be huge.

I push the hoe deep into the dirt and wiggle it back and forth, enough to loosen the earth but not enough to upset the soil's invisible creatures.

There's a whole underground world down there that I had never thought about before. The bacteria that live close to the surface can't live deeper down, and the ones deeper down can't survive close to the surface. Each creature has a job to do. If someone mixes them all up by digging, a whole lot of them die, and the rest have to regroup before they can get back to work.

Uli nods at the row of cabbages. "Looks good. Next task. Turning the compost."

"Aye, aye, captain." I salute him with one dirty-gloved hand. He smiles, and I wander over to the big wood-and-chicken-wire boxes behind the greenhouse. A wave of warm air rushes up to me when I lift the lid. It smells like soil after a rain. I dig the hoe in deep, haul out dirt from the bottom and bury the eggshells and other kitchen scraps that were resting on top.

"Asparagus should be ready to eat this year," Uli says.

"Blech," I say.

"You'll change your mind. I planted it three years ago. This'll be the first crop."

"Wait." I turn to face him. "You've spent three years on a vegetable that tastes like socks and makes your pee smell funny?"

He grins. "Not socks! Asparagus tastes like Heaven. No comparison to—"

"I know, I know. Organic heirlooms always taste better than conventional store-bought food, right?" I smile so he'll know I'm not about to bite his head off like Dad would. Sometimes I wonder if the organic debate is what finally ripped my family apart. I mean, Dad did a lot of the cooking when he was a teenager. Imagine coming home from school, cooking dinner and then eating to the soundtrack of *The Dangers of Conventionally Grown Food*. I picture plates flying, organic gravy dripping down the wall and my dad secretly stocking Uli's freezer with TV dinners just out of spite.

Uli props his elbows on his knees and takes a deep breath. "Your father must have had a rough day yesterday. He sure was touchy last night."

"Yeah, no kidding." He's been grumpy for a week straight but won't tell me why. *Grown-up stuff*, is all he says. That could mean anything from money to Mom to Estelle with a whole new list of stuff to fix in the building. Today when I got home, Dad was stomping around, slamming cupboards, because the power had been out since the morning. All day people had been knocking on his door to let him know. His bad mood filled the apartment, so I went to see if Nikko was up for a wobble around the school parking lot. But he was out, so I came over to Uli's, leaving Dad to deal with his own mood. "He's not exactly an open book, my dad."

"You got that right," my grandfather says.

I close the lid of the compost and go back to where Uli's sitting. I pull out a tiny chickweed plant from between the spinach and hand it to him. "What's next?"

"The bed over there needs weeding." He pops the chickweed into his mouth, points to a jungle of weeds at the far end and picks up his stool. We make our way over there, and he says, "Now tell me what's new with your Montreal friend."

He likes my Sofia stories. Last time I was here, I told him about her upcycling sewing class and the funky purple trim she added to an old polyester dress. When she went to put it on, she discovered she'd sewn the sleeves shut.

"Nothing new today," I tell him, "except that our favorite DVD store closed. Me and Sofia were loyal customers, maybe the only customers. No one rents movies anymore. But the guy who owned the store loved movies, and he gave the best recommendations." I try to picture our neighborhood without Película, but I can't.

"It's hard to see a place change," Uli says, like he's reading my mind. He bends down to pluck a few blades of grass from the soil but then sits back on his stool, as if the effort is too much for him.

It must be hard to see himself change too, I think. We're silent for a few minutes. It's a comfortable silence though.

"What's that?"

I stop weeding for a moment, and I hear it too, a bicycle bell ringing over and over again. "I'll go look."

It's Nikko. The saddlebags on his bike and the box on the back rack are brimming with ice-cream cartons. "Jackpot!" he says. "Your grandfather around?"

"Is all that ice cream for him?" Does Uli even like ice cream? Sure, we ate it together in Montreal once, but I've never seen him eat it here. It's packaged food, after all.

"It's for everyone!" He tells me how the grocery store's freezer conked out in the power outage, so they were selling it for a dollar a tub. "I bought enough for Uli and for everyone in the building. It's half melted, but ice cream is ice cream, right?"

Uli appears behind me. "Deep freezer is in the basement. Toss it all in there. Firm it up a bit before you hand it out. I'll keep a few tubs for myself. Thanks."

"Really?" I ask. "All this talk about organic and local, and now you're going to fill your freezer with this stuff?"

"Bah," Uli says. "Ice cream's not about nutrition. It'll have more flavor in my mouth than in a trash bin, which is where it would have ended up if Nikko hadn't bought it."

"My thinking precisely," says Nikko.

"Gotta pick your battles," Uli continues. "I choose chocolate. Basement door is this way."

A few minutes later, the freezer is full. We make our way back to the greenhouse and stretch a plastic tablecloth over the potting table. Uli brings out bowls and spoons from his kitchen. Each bowl gets filled to the brim.

"You've got a big garden, Uli," Nikko says as we scoop the sweet coldness into our mouths. "I bet it's a lot of work."

The garden is still not much to look at—a few plants are poking up out of the dirt rows between all the plastic bottles sticking up everywhere—and I wonder what Nikko really thinks of the place. "Uli grows endangered vegetables," I blurt out, because suddenly it feels important that Nikko doesn't think my grandfather is as weird as I did at first. "He's been collecting the seeds for decades. If it weren't for him, a lot of these plants would die out completely."

Uli smiles at me before turning to Nikko. "The garden has to be big for a good harvest of seeds. Vegetables grow in the meantime. Too many for me to eat. I donate most to the soup kitchen."

"Really?" I didn't know that part.

Nikko asks which soup kitchen, Uli mentions a name, and Nikko nods like he's heard of it. "I volunteer at the one on Pandora," he says.

I didn't know that either. "What do you do there?"

"I work in the kitchen." He waves his spoon through the air like it's a sword. "The fastest chopper in the west. That's me."

"Good skill to have," Uli says. "You come over when we're canning this summer. We could use your help."

"At your service." He nods his head graciously.

"So do you grow the same plants every year?" Nikko asks.

"At least two of each variety," Uli says. "I usually try for more, but space is at a premium."

"I'm sure no one would blame you for skipping a season," I say.

"I would blame me," Uli says. "Every region used to have its own vegetables. Peru still has hundreds of varieties of corn and potatoes. But the unusual ones will all become extinct unless people keep planting them. The whole world becomes poorer when that happens."

Nikko has a thoughtful look on his face. "So this garden is a museum too. A living vegetable museum."

"Exactly." Uli smiles and looks over at me. I can tell he approves of my new long-haired friend. "Now, who wants more ice cream?"

"Are you kidding?" Nikko asks. "I couldn't eat another spoonful."

"Last call," Uli warns, but I shake my head too.

"I'll take these inside." Nikko begins collecting bowls and spoons.

"Leave 'em," Uli says. "Go hand out your ice cream."

I pull on my gardening gloves. "Will you tell people you rescued it from the trash?"

"Sure," Nikko says. "Who's going to care? And if they do, that's more for us. Wanna help?"

I look over at Uli. "I—"

"Go ahead," Uli says. "Weeding can wait. And maybe I'll come too. I'll bring some maple-walnut over to William." William is Uli's friend in our building. They've known each other forever.

Nikko takes his bike home. Uli and I start loading the ice cream from the freezer into a couple of empty boxes he has lying around. "Nice young man."

"I bet you say that about everyone who shows up with gallons of ice cream."

He smiles. "Glad he was thinking straight. Imagine throwing out food! You'd never catch me doing that. If you've ever been truly hungry, you just can't do it."

"You were hungry a lot growing up?" I ask.

"I used to eat paper when I was little, just to fill my belly. I never told my mother that though. She tried so hard to look after me. Later I lived on the streets for a while after leaving my uncle's place. I was always glad when people threw out food then. I got a good few meals from dumpsters. You can't be too persnickety when you're on the street." He shifts a few tubs in the freezer. "There! There's one! Maple-walnut!"

I go in after it, and when I hand the carton to him, he holds it in the air triumphantly. Nikko comes down the basement steps and lifts one of the boxes. I grab the other, and we parade across the street to our building. We say goodbye to my grandfather at the elevator. I would hug him, but I'm carrying a box loaded with ice cream.

"Will you come again tomorrow?" he asks.

I nod. "Sure, I'll finish up that weeding. And maybe some more ice cream."

"Deal," he says.

First stop is our apartment's little freezer. "Ice-cream rescuers get first pick," Nikko says, and I choose dark chocolate and French vanilla, hoping Dad will make some of his amazing strawberry sauce for sundaes. He's not home—which must mean he's running off his bad mood, thank goodness—so we head up to the fourth floor and work our way down. Nikko does most of the talking because he knows everybody. Everyone greets us as if we were the smartest, most generous people ever.

The one door we don't knock on is Estelle's.

Nikko says there's no point because she'll either be offended that the ice cream is half melted, or she'll complain that we didn't get the kind she likes. I go along with this right up until we're almost out of ice cream, but the whole time I keep thinking of that day in second grade when Lisa Sampton invited our entire class to her birthday party except for Billy Odiah, who smelled funny, and me, the teacher's kid. No matter how annoying Estelle can be, I can't offer ice cream to everyone in the building and leave her out. Within seconds of knocking on her door, though, I wish I'd listened to Nikko.

"I certainly don't need the calories," says Estelle. She takes the carton anyway and squints at the label. "And I hope you used your discretion when it came to William on fourth. He has a heart condition. Every gram of fat puts him at risk. I, for one—"

Nikko raises a hand and sets off down the hall. "Sorry, Mrs. Fornan. We won't endanger your life any further. Gotta go now! Bye!"

I hesitate for a moment, then give an awkward little wave and dash after Nikko. As soon as we're in the stairwell, he says, "If you ever bring me ice cream and I act like you're a public menace, please lob the tub at my head."

I imagine the gooey mess dribbling down his shoulders. "Do you have a flavor preference?"

"Blue bubble gum would look rather dashing, wouldn't it?"

He follows me down to my apartment. He had planned to head home after we delivered to Estelle—his apartment is across the hall from hers—but I guess striding away from Estelle to fumble with a key in his own lock wouldn't have been a very grand exit. He waves a spare carton of raspberry-ripple at me. "Want this last tub of poison?"

"Sure. I'll stuff it in the freezer."

We open the fire door into our hallway just as two paramedics and a firefighter squeeze out of the elevator, rolling a stretcher between them.

"Uh-oh," says Nikko.

I recognize Uli's white hair first. I scream and run to him. No reaction. One paramedic glances at me but says nothing.

"Is he—?"

William is the last one out of the elevator. "He's alive, Chloë. But he had another stroke. I called the ambulance."

"Can I go with him?"

William tells the paramedics that I'm the granddaughter.

"Sorry, honey," one of them says. "You need to be over eighteen to ride in the wagon."

"But where are you taking him?" I don't know any of the hospitals here. And where's my dad?

Dad shows up just as the ambulance takes off. I'm freaking out in the hallway, and William is hugging me with his frail arms. Nikko is standing off to the side, looking at his feet.

SEVEN

I've never seen Dad drive so fast. We screech into the Emergency parking lot. Dad's swearing as he tries to find his wallet to pay for parking. "Why do they make you pay for parking?" he shouts. "Isn't it bad enough to have someone in Emergency?"

The woman at the front desk won't let us see Uli right away. She says she'll call us as soon as they're ready for us. Dad paces back and forth in front of the blue vinyl chairs. I slump into mine, fists clenched in my pockets, staring down at the floor. Every two minutes Dad walks over to the counter, and finally the woman stands up and says the doctor will see us now, as if we're in a clinic to see about a runny nose or an upset stomach.

She leads us through heavy doors with a sign saying *No admittance beyond this point.* We pass an old, old woman in a stretcher pushed up against one wall of the short hallway. A few feet farther along, a man with a short brown beard, a white coat and a stethoscope around his neck is waiting for us. "You're Ulrich Becher's son?"

Dad nods, and he grips my hand as if I'm a little kid again. Or maybe as if he's a little kid again.

"I'm Dr. Yanofski." The doctor takes Dad by the elbow and leads him to a chair. He brings another for me. "I'm afraid I don't have good news for you. Your father had another stroke on the way to the hospital. A big one. I'm afraid he didn't survive. But it was all over quite quickly. He didn't suffer."

I freeze. Then my heart starts pounding. Dad's crying, sobbing as if he's going to split in two.

Uli is dead.

It doesn't make any sense. I just saw him an hour ago. We were talking, and he was serving ice cream, and…

"…take you to see him…"

Somewhere behind us, someone screams, and people are shouting, but I don't even care.

"…sorry for your loss…"

My father stands up, then wipes my cheeks with the back of his fingers. I didn't know they were wet.

"…see the body…" he says.

"I can't," I say.

"It's important," he says. "It's part of saying goodbye."

I shake my head.

A few steps away, the doctor has stopped, waiting next to a closed curtain. My dad takes a deep, shaky breath, squeezes both of my hands and talks to me quietly. "I understand, Chloë. I didn't want to see my mom's body either. I told Dad that I wanted to remember her healthy. But he insisted. He said everyone's scared of death, but it's part of life. If we face it head-on, we change our relationship with it."

I don't say anything. *Please don't make me do this.*

"I'm not going to force you," Dad says. "But I want you to know that it wasn't scary. When my mom was sick, I saw her suffer every single day. But when I saw her body, I knew that the suffering was over. Her body was just...her body. She wasn't in there anymore. That was important for me." He looks at me, squeezes my hands again and turns to go.

I see him reach the curtain. He's about to go in, leaving me back here, alone.

No way.

Curtains. Blankets. Uli's mouth is open. His skin is yellowish gray.

And Dad's right. There's nothing more final than this.

My clock radio says *10:12 AM*. My first thought is that my history report is due today. I haven't even started it. I pull my pillow over my head. What seems like seconds later, Dad is knocking on my door. He comes in holding a paper bag from the Mexican place downtown, the one we used to go to with Uli. Yesterday comes crashing back in on me.

The sirens. The emergency room. The doctor. Uli's body. The horribly silent ride home.

"It's after noon." Dad's eyes are red and puffy. "You should eat something."

"I don't want to."

"Do it anyway." His voice is gentle but firm, like when I was a kid and I was screaming because my knee was full of gravel and he had to wash it out. I take the bag from him, open it up and will myself not to gag as I eat one of the burritos Uli liked so much.

"I guess I'm not going to school today," I say after my first bite. Suddenly I'm ravenous.

"I'll send a note. Your teachers will understand."

He sits on my bed. I eat in silence for a few minutes. I can't think about the food because then I'll think of Uli. I can't think about my history report because not handing it in makes me think of Uli. I can't think of anything, so I look at the floor and chew.

"Are you okay?" Dad asks.

Uli's dead. My grandfather that I'd only started to get to know. One fifth of my family is dead. "Am I okay? What kind of question is that?"

"I don't know," he says. "I just want you to be okay. I want a magic wand to wave so that nothing will ever hurt you again." His eyes fill with tears.

I squeeze mine shut. The tears spill out anyway, but at least I can't see Dad crying. The only thing worse than feeling like I'm going to shatter into a million pieces is knowing that Dad feels the same way.

The smooth stones on the beach remind me of the ones lining Uli's garden beds. Maybe he collected them from right where I'm standing, years ago or maybe months ago, when his legs still obeyed him.

To think that only a few months ago, I barely thought about my grandfather at all. I was thousands of miles away, hanging out with Sofia, going to school, knitting and dreaming of weekends. All that time, he was here, growing a garden of foods that kept other people's family memories alive. But what about our family memories? Why did I have to wait until I was thirteen to get to know Uli? Why did I have to wait so long to find out there was an apple tree that connects me, Dad and Uli to a tree that grew a long time ago in Poland, a tree that Uli used to swing in as a kid?

I toss a stone into the water. And then another. I think about the muscles in my arm that shoot each rock into the air, and about Uli's good arm that will never throw a rock again. Then I'm running, sprinting flat out as if I could leave yesterday behind. I run up the stairs from the beach and along the path that follows the water. A few blocks later I pass the Stop sign wrapped in red, yellow and green wool that sparked the first real conversation I had with my grandfather. A driver slams on his brakes and yells something out the window, but I keep running until I'm back on our street under the cherry trees. I can hardly breathe anymore. I slow to a walk, through Uli's front gate and into his garden. It's the only place I want to be right now. I wish I'd gotten here years sooner.

I look across the rows of dirt at the greenhouse. I half expect him to stand up behind the potting table to pick up the ice-cream dishes that are still stacked there from yesterday. A museum, Nikko called it. To preserve memories. The last link I have with someone I wish I'd known my whole life.

I crouch down by the garden bed near the house and yank handfuls of weeds from the dirt. As if sticking to yesterday's plan could somehow bring my grandfather back.

"Tell me something happy," I tell Sofia. It's Saturday morning. I'm sitting on my bed, knitting her a hat. Sofia's sitting on her bed, designing a costume for a school play. Other than the laptop cameras and the thousands of miles between us, this is like Saturday mornings used to be. I knit, and she draws or sews.

"I'm not going to tell you something happy," she says. "You tell me what happened."

I knit mechanically, eyes on the yarn, and manage to tell her about Uli in fits and starts, with long moments of crying and sniffling in between. Sofia says my name. I look up, and she's not drawing anymore. She's staring right into the screen. She's crying too. "I'm sorry, Chloë. I wish I was there."

"Me too." I take a few deep breaths and wipe my tears away. "I can't decide if I wish we'd never moved here, or if I wish it had happened sooner." I hope Sofia knows what I mean. I wish I'd had more time with Uli.

"I'm glad you got to meet him," she says.

"Me too." I pick up my knitting again. She looks at me for a few seconds longer, then reaches for her pencil. We don't say anything for a while. I need to talk about something else, something lighter. "Remember Slater?"

"The kid across the street with the rat and the attitude problem?"

"Yeah, that one," I say. "I found out why he tries to make everyone's life miserable."

"It's not because he's a loser?"

I shrug. "This kid in my math class says he used to go to the most expensive private school in the city. Then something happened, his parents sold their place, and they moved across town to a dumpy little house on this street. Now he's going to public school like everyone else."

"That's so sweet!" she says. "You've got matching stories!"

"What?" I never would have seen it that way, but I guess she has a point. "I don't try to get back at the world by bullying everyone around me though. And I'm sure he didn't move here because his dad got fired for freaking out at a student. His dad's an accountant or something."

"Both of you were bitter about having to move though."

"But it's not so bad here." The words are out of my mouth before I can think about them.

Sofia stops with her pencil midair and looks into the camera. "Did you just say what I think you said?"

"I mean, it's not Montreal. That's for sure. But it doesn't pretend to be either. I can go to the beach here every day if I want."

"We've got beaches here too," she says. "And they're sand, not rock."

"Yeah, but here I can go all year-round, and sometimes I don't see a soul."

"And that's a good thing?"

"Sometimes," I say. "When I want to get away from it all."

Sofia says nothing and goes back to drawing for a few seconds. "Do you think you're going to stay there?" She's not looking at me. I flash back to the night before I left. She was crying, convinced I'd never move back.

"You can't get rid of me that easily," I say. "I like it here more than I did before, but it's still not home. I haven't had a decent bagel since I left Montreal."

"Now that's more like it." She grins and holds up her sketch. "So what do you think I should do with this neckline?"

Uli didn't leave any instructions, so Dad chooses cremation. The idea creeps me out until he reminds me that burial usually involves pumping the body full of chemicals and sticking it into the ground. Not a good option for an organic gardener.

"Tell me you're not planning to keep the ashes in a vase on the bookshelf," I say. I've heard of people doing this. It's ten kinds of creepy. "Maybe we can mix them into the soil beneath the apple tree. Isn't ash good for the soil?"

"No way," Dad says.

"It's not?"

"I don't know. I'm saying, no, we're not putting the ashes under the apple tree."

"Why not? He loved that apple tree. Did you know he—?"

Dad shakes his head. "I know the whole story, believe me. But I don't want his ashes there. Someday that house is going to be sold. How are we going to feel if they bulldoze the whole thing, rip out the tree and build something new?"

"Sold?" I hadn't thought about that. "I guess you're right."

Dad doesn't want a memorial service either. He says he's up to his eyeballs with sorting through Uli's stuff and talking to lawyers about the will. The last thing he wants is to organize a public event. "My father never went to church anyway. He'd hate the idea of some random preacher up there talking about him."

"You're wimping out," I say.

Mom agrees, arguing through the laptop on the kitchen counter. She's wearing a silvery blouse I don't recognize and dangly earrings, as if she dressed up for this conversation. Behind her, our houseplants look as brown and droopy as ever. But Mom herself is different. She's more focused than I've seen her in a long time. "Look, Darryl, yes, you had unfinished business with Uli, but this is your last chance. You need to do something to say goodbye."

Dad keeps stirring the pot of spaghetti sauce. "But who do I invite? William on fourth? Did he have any other friends?"

"Dad! Uli lived here for fifty years! He had a garden full of seeds that people gave him. Of course he had other friends!"

"But I've never met any of those people."

"You never asked to either," I snap back. Dad keeps stirring. Mom watches from inside the screen.

"I bet he had an address book somewhere."

"I wouldn't know where to look," says Dad. "If you saw his place, you'd know what I mean."

"You've been in there?" I ask. "Recently?"

"Yesterday."

I spin around, open the fridge and rummage inside so my parents won't see me scrubbing the tears from my face. All these weeks, I only ever saw Uli's garden and basement. I never went into his house to have tea with him or to sit around playing a board game. Or to do any of those normal grandparent-grandkid things.

My parents keep talking. Eventually Dad takes the spoon out of the sauce and puts the lid on the pot. "Okay, okay. We'll find the address book. I'll ask William for some ideas about who to invite too."

"Let me know when you've got a date," Mom says, "so I can book my flights."

"Really?" I almost smile. Almost. It will be good to have Mom here. As if the three of us are a family again, for a few days anyway.

After that I guess the waiting will be over. It's finally clear what will happen next—clear out the house, put it up for sale and move back to Montreal for good. It doesn't make sense to stay now that Uli's gone, right? I should feel relieved to be heading home. So why do I feel the opposite?

EIGHT

The church doesn't look anything like a church. It's a yellow house on a quiet residential street—no steeple, no parking lot. Inside, it's bright, with big windows and maybe a hundred wooden chairs, set up in horseshoe rows. No crosses, no hymn books, not even any Bibles that I can see.

William was the one who suggested this place. He calls it a meeting house, and he's allowed to invite us to have the memorial here because he's a member of the Religious Society of Friends. I told Dad it sounds like a cult, but he just laughed and said it's another name for the Quakers, an old and well-respected branch of Christianity.

"The Quakers still exist?" I asked, picturing William and dozens of other people sitting around in funny hats like the guy on the oatmeal package.

"They do," Dad said, "and if you're thinking of the oatmeal, don't worry. They wear modern clothes now. They get together to meditate. Sometimes people stand up to speak if they feel it would be useful. Uli went a few times. He knew lots of people there through William, and he liked the quiet."

So here we are. Nikko and I are the youngest by far. My parents are next.

They're making a big effort this weekend. Mom's been here almost twelve hours, and I haven't heard a single angry word between them. Dad and I picked her up at the airport at midnight. Mom travels a lot, but whenever we picked her up at the airport in Montreal, she'd be in stretchy pants and a comfy sweatshirt. Last night she was wearing tight, stylish jeans and a purple, wraparound sweater. Dad did a double take, but I don't know if Mom noticed. She was going on about how much I'd grown and how she liked my hair tied back. Eventually, she let go of me, hugged him and said he looked good, that he'd lost weight. He smiled. Things were starting off well.

Now here we are in a Quaker meeting house packed with people. Dad was shocked when he realized how many people Uli kept in touch with. We've spent weeks letting people know about this memorial service.

"Chloë, could you set up the photos, please?" Dad hands me a display board and points me to an easel in the far corner. I squeeze through the crowd to arrange the four pictures Dad rummaged out of a box this week. The first is black-and-white: a small boy in shorts holding the hand of a woman in a kerchief. I think of Uli's story about the apple tree. That's my great-grandmother, who escaped with Uli in her arms, saved the seeds and died before she could get to Canada. I wish I'd asked Uli if I look like her. I've squinted at her until my eyes hurt, but the picture's too small for spotting any resemblance.

In the next photo, the little boy has grown to a man. He's wearing a suit and standing beside a woman in a wedding dress. My grandmother Gwen. I don't know how they met. Dad says he doesn't know either. (How did he go forty years without thinking to ask?) Dad's in the next photograph, a baby in his mother's arms.

The last picture is of me with Uli, at a Tibetan restaurant the week before he died. I remember groaning when my grandfather asked my father to take the picture. My hair had been stuffed in a hat all afternoon. I had a soup stain on my shirt. But I'm so glad Dad didn't listen to me. Uli's arm looks awkward around my shoulders, and even though he was usually serious around my dad, he has an almost goofy grin on his face. It's a good picture. Our last one together.

Four generations of my family. Dad and I are the only ones still alive. We should have more photos. I should have more stories. How can we pretend to celebrate Uli's life if this is all we have to show of it? Why didn't I ever take a picture of him in his garden?

"I am so very sorry for your loss."

I turn. William holds out his bony, gnarled fingers. It occurs to me that Uli and William were about as different as two people could be. Uli must have towered over his friend, for one thing. This small man is always very neatly dressed in a collared shirt and pants. He's so formal and polite, compared to Uli's gruffness. I wonder what they talked about all those years.

I let go of his hand and remember his frail arms around me when the paramedics carried Uli to the ambulance. I blink hard. "I'm sorry for your loss, too, William. You knew him better than I did."

"That too is a loss, my dear. Your grandfather was a fine man. Not a perfect one—no one ever is— but a fine man nonetheless. I do hope you got to see some of that in him in your short time together."

I swallow and look away. I want to be back in Montreal. Back in a time years ago, when my parents were still happy and before I knew my grandfather. A time where I didn't know what I was missing and what I was about to lose.

"I'm sorry." William squeezes my hand in both of his and then makes his way to the line of chairs.

I stand there wishing the floor would open up and swallow me whole. Mom places a vase of flowers on a little table next to my mostly dead family, and as if she's read my mind, she offers me a reason to escape into the kitchen. By the time Nikko and I have the coffee mugs lined up and go back to the main room, most people are already seated. Nikko and I find a place to sit, too, in the front row, next to my parents.

A thin, old man in a powder-blue suit stands to welcome everyone. He explains that we're here to honor Uli with quiet meditation but that we're welcome to offer a story if we feel led to do so. He sits down again. Everyone is quiet.

Most people have their heads bowed. I do, too, but I sneak looks around the room. I wonder if any of the people who gave him seeds will stand up to tell a story. I can hear people shifting in their chairs and my father breathing next to me. I fidget. The silence feels like we're all waiting for something to happen.

Finally Dad stands up. At first, he hadn't planned to speak: *What would I say? That Dad and I didn't see eye to eye on most things? Everyone there probably knows that already.* But then a few days ago, Dad started worrying. *What if no one says anything? What if we sit there for a whole hour, and no one has anything to say? That would be the worst send-off ever.*

I guess Dad's decided to get the ball rolling. He clears his throat. I close my eyes to listen.

"My father began planting vegetables the summer my mother died."

My eyes spring open. I look up at my father, standing next to me. He's never talked about his mother dying. I only know it was cancer because I asked Mom. Now he's sharing with a roomful of strangers a story he's never shared with me.

I see Mom slip her hand into his, something I haven't seen her do in years.

"I was eleven," Dad continues. "My father brought home some seeds and said we needed to plant them."

I wonder who the seeds came from. Were they a gift, or did he get them at a gardening shop or grocery store, like most people do?

"We dug up the whole lawn and planted rows of carrots, peas, lettuce, green beans—and a pumpkin," Dad says, smiling. "A huge pumpkin that weighed almost as much as I did. There's a picture of it somewhere."

I never knew he helped with the garden. By the smile on his face, I can tell he enjoyed it too.

"Gardening was what my dad and I did together to heal. He told me we needed to grow something, to add new life to a year that had been all about sickness and death."

Like Uli had done with the apple seeds after he watched his mother die.

"For as long as I lived in that house, that garden was a place where I could go to think and just be. We worked side by side for hours, sometimes talking, but lots of times just being quiet together. That garden was where he taught me that even when everything feels too hard to bear, good things can grow."

I never imagined my dad working in Uli's garden and loving it just as much as my grandfather did. But I'm glad to know now. I like picturing them there together. I wish I knew what happened to change all that.

Dad sits down. A few people smile at him. He nods back. I wonder why he's never told me any of this before. Did he always know he felt that way about the garden, or is it something he's just figuring out now?

A woman behind us stands up and talks about meeting Uli years ago at the diner where she worked. Right away I know who she is. It's the woman who gave him the cucamelon seeds. A man in a wheelchair tells how Uli brought him tomato sauce every summer and sometimes wheeled him over to the garden, just to sit close to the tomatoes that his mother used to grow. One after another, people stand to tell everyone just how much Uli meant to them, how he cared about little things that other people didn't bother with. He paid attention to details and was a great listener. That starts Dad crying again. Mom puts her arm around him. He leans into her. I put a hand on his knee. He grips it just as hard as he did in the hospital.

Nikko glances sideways at me. I try to smile back to show I'm okay, but I doubt it's very convincing, because I'm crying at the same time.

Story after story about seeds, memories, little kindnesses and the garden. Every story involves the living museum behind his house, which will one day be sold and maybe bulldozed to make room for something new. It's the worst kind of end for a museum. Part of me almost wishes we could stay in Victoria, just to look after the garden and make sure the plants live on.

NINE

I've kept checking in on the garden since Uli died. Every few days, I go over to weed, turn the compost and water the tomatoes in the greenhouse. I found a few more packets of seeds a few weeks ago, looked up online when to plant each one and made myself a little planting calendar that I've been following. Corn mid-May. Cucumbers early June. I don't know why I bother, because it's not like we're staying here. But it felt wrong not to. I couldn't bear to watch the tomatoes die or the little plants get overtaken with weeds now that my grandfather's gone.

I need to find the seed collection. If I can do that, then maybe someone else can carry on Uli's work, no matter what happens to the house. The vegetables aren't attached to that particular patch of land. Anyone can grow them, and isn't that exactly what Uli would want? For more people to care about them?

I don't know where he put it. Those little packets of seeds on the kitchen counter are the only ones I've found so far, but I haven't looked very hard either. I will now though. I have to. For Uli.

Over the next few weeks, I help my dad sort through Uli's things. Today, while Dad fumbles for his keys, I spot Slater sitting on his steps next door, playing with his rat. I'm pretending not to notice him, but then a short old man slams out of the house. "Back at five," I hear him say to Slater. "Heat up the lasagna your mother left in the fridge, okay?"

"Heat it up yourself," Slater snaps.

The old man slams his car door and drives away. I look at Dad. He shrugs and lets us into the house. Walking into Uli's living room is like stepping back in time: worn, red shag rug, orange lampshades, avocado-green couch. Even the books on the shelves look old. Each time we come over, I start searching for the seed collection. But Dad is only ever here for a few minutes before he suddenly remembers something that needs urgent attention back at the building. And he won't let me stay here alone. Yesterday he planned to spend the whole day in Uli's basement, sorting, but when I got home from school, he was scrubbing moss from our front walk with something that looked like a toothbrush. He even launched into a speech about why this was the perfect tool for the job. I told him to quit stalling.

I get why it's hard for him though. First he has to deal with all the memories. Then he has to deal with all the junk. The entire basement is crammed with rows and rows of shelves, stacked with boxes of—not family treasures, but rags, newspapers and even cardboard toilet-paper rolls. This afternoon I'm determined to keep Dad here long enough for me to find that old shoebox full of seeds, stories and maps. I'll look in every single box in the basement, I think. But after two hours I've thrown everything I've come across into the "garbage" pile. (Everything except for Uli's impressive elastic-band collection, that is. It's a ball of bands the size of a small watermelon. In my whole life, I don't think I'll need that many elastics, but if I do, I'm ready. In the meantime, maybe Nikko and I can toss it around at the park or something.)

"Look at this!" Dad says.

I expect to turn and see him holding up a framed photo or a favorite book from when he was a kid. Instead he's got a fistful of colored cords, all different lengths, none longer than my arm. "What's that?"

"My rope collection! I wonder if I remember..." He's sitting cross-legged on the floor now, twisting a green cord into a complicated knot. "I do! Look at that! It's an Ashley stopper knot. That's how you make sure the rope doesn't slide through a hole."

"You collected cords...to practice knots?" I've heard of some weird hobbies, but as Uli would have said, this one takes the cake.

"Here's another." Dad grabs two cords, yellow and blue, and ties their ends together in a complicated way. "An alpine butterfly bend!"

I like seeing him there, looking happy for the first time since he stepped into this house. I can't stand being inside anymore, though, especially since I've run out of places to look for the seed collection. "Can I go tidy up the garden?"

We both know it doesn't need any tidying. I've been here almost every day since Uli died, and the place is spotless. Dad hasn't said anything. I think he gets why I keep working on it.

"Chloë," he says, putting down his cords, "I need to talk to you about that. You're going to have to start thinking about letting the garden go. The longer you hold on, the more painful it will be to say goodbye."

"But it needs looking after," I say. "No one's going to buy a place with a weed pit in the back."

He frowns. "Chloë, it's not going to be sold right away, I don't think."

What is he talking about? Isn't he selling this place so we can both move back to Montreal? Didn't he say we shouldn't put Uli's ashes under the tree because someone might take the tree down when the place is sold? "You said—"

"I know," he says. "Look, I haven't been totally upfront with you about this, but I guess you're going to find out soon enough. This house didn't belong to Uli."

"What?" That doesn't make sense. Why would he plant a tree in front of a rental? And create an enormous food garden full of valuable endangered plants?

"I'm sorry," Dad says. "I should have told you sooner. But watching you looking after the garden and putting so much time into it...I didn't know how to tell you."

I don't know what to say. "When...how long do we—?"

"We're paid up for a few more weeks. Then it'll go back to the landlord." My dad is looking down at the floor. "He'll probably renovate before he rents it out to anyone else, but either way, he's not going to want either of us on his property after June 1. I—"

I stop listening. I want to stick my fingers in my ears and run away. What else is he not telling me, and why is everyone in this family so secretive? Where did Uli hide that seed collection? How am I going to find it? It was bad enough when I didn't have a time limit, but now I know I only have a few weeks to save my grandfather's life's work.

I take a deep breath, but it doesn't help. Nothing does.

"Película is being turned into a Mongolian Hot Pot," Sofia says. "The owner's son is in my class."

I groan. "Another restaurant? But that place is one of the best parts of the neighborhood!"

"The neighborhood is changing, Chloë. You'll hardly recognize it when you come home."

"I bet," I say. "It'll be weird going back."

"You're going to miss Victoria, aren't you?" Sofia's voice is soft.

"Yeah," I say. "I can really see why Uli moved here now, and why Dad wanted to move back. I wish I could be in two places at once."

"Done." Dad locks Uli's door and pats the frame. For three solid weeks, he's been sorting, selling and saving things, stuffing keepsakes into our storage locker. I've looked everywhere for the seeds. You'd think that a man who labeled everything from toilet rolls to elastic bands would have made a special effort with this particular item. But I've combed every last inch of that property. Nothing.

"Goodbye, old house," Dad says. "Goodbye, garden." He turns to look at me. He asked me to collect all the gardening tools and the plastic bottles Uli used for watering a while ago. I never did. So he just left them. Maybe he figures the landlord won't care.

"I'm not saying goodbye to the garden yet," I say. "I'm going to ask the landlord if I can look after it until they get new tenants. If they're doing renos, we might even get a full summer's harvest, and we could save the seeds from the crops. Uli explained how." I tell Dad that Nikko's agreed to look after things when we leave for Montreal and is also looking for other people who like growing weird vegetables. "You know what Nikko's like with research. I'm sure we'll—"

"No."

"What? Why not?" I ask. "Why would the landlord care if—"

Dad shakes his head. "I know this is hard on you, Chloë. Everything's shifting, and now I'm asking you to give up yet another place you care about. But you have to trust me on this one. You've got to let this go. The longer you hold on, the worse it'll be."

"You don't get it," I say. If Dad had been around when Uli was telling stories about every last plant—who he'd got the seeds from, and where they came from before that—this wouldn't be a place only I care about. "If I can harvest the seeds and give them to someone who wants them, then Uli's work won't go to waste."

"Chloë," he says firmly, "it's over. I hate to say it, but it's over. Your grandfather is gone. Nothing we can do will bring him back."

"But it's not just about him! It's about what he believed in—what he lived for! That's all we have left of him, and you won't even let me have that?" I take off down the sidewalk.

Dad calls me back, but I keep going.

"Do you know who the landlord is?" Nikko asks when I tell him the whole story. It's late evening, and we're pedaling home from my longest bike ride yet. He's been checking out free piles—stuff that people have piled by the sidewalk—so tonight we're riding home with three extra bike tires, two cookbooks, a bagful of yarn and a mug with a smiling carrot on it.

"My dad probably knows the landlord," I say, "but I doubt he'll give me details. He says I need to let go. Maybe I can check with City Hall? They must keep a record of who owns what."

"What about talking to William?" Nikko suggests. "He knew your grandfather. He might remember the landlord's name. Heck, he might even have the seed collection."

I let out a whoop. "Why didn't I think of that?" Uli probably gave it to William for safekeeping. It makes perfect sense.

"Maybe we can visit him tomorrow," Nikko says. "He's always asking me to run errands for him, and he always invites me in for tea afterward. He'd love having an extra visitor, I'm sure."

On the sidewalk, someone whistles. "Well, if it isn't the Fashion Disaster and the Bedbug Queen! A white-trash romance!"

I glance at Nikko. "Someone let the neighborhood chimp out of his cage."

"What did you say?" Slater shouts and darts in front of us. I slam on the brakes. (I should have run him over.) Two guys step onto the street beside him. The short, freckled one is Griffin from my math class, trying to look tough with his arms crossed over his chest. But I see fear in his eyes. The guy in the baseball cap, I've never seen before. He grabs my handlebars.

"Let go!" I shout over the pounding of my heart. Okay, maybe I don't shout it, but I'm sure he heard me. He doesn't let go though.

"She said, *let go*," Nikko says. "Are you deaf?"

And Slater's on him. Nikko's bike crashes to the ground, but Baseball Cap pulls Slater off before he can throw a punch. "Jeez, man! Not here!"

Griffin shoots me a panicked do-something look, so I scream, the loudest helpless-girl scream I can muster. Griffin takes off. A second later so do Baseball Cap and Slater.

A front door opens. The woman looks up and down the street. "You okay out there?"

Nikko gets up, dusts himself off and waves at her. "We're fine, ma'am. Just fell off my bike. Thanks for checking."

"Okay. You might want to walk your bike with that load. Glad you're all right." She waves and closes the door again.

"Friend of yours?" Nikko asks.

I shake my head. "I've never seen her before. I—"

"I meant the thug who attacked me." He smiles the same kind of I'm-hurting-but-please-don't-worry-about-me smile that I gave him at the memorial. His elbows are bloody and dripping.

Both of our bikes are on the ground. I pick up his and hold it out to him. "Can you ride?"

We pedal slowly home. "Maybe I should take up kickboxing," he says.

"Thanks for sticking up for me," I say quietly.

He launches into an extra-sappy version of "That's What Friends Are For." I laugh and join in. I'm going to miss Nikko when we're gone.

TEN

Sofia has texted me a few times today, but I haven't answered. Some stories shouldn't be told in a limited number of characters. I can't text *Attacked by thug* from math class. I'll tell her over the phone, when it all feels more yesterday.

Nikko looks fine when I visit him after school. His elbows are bandaged, and he's careful about bending them, but that's it.

"What did your parents say?" I ask when we're safely out in the hallway.

"Dad told me not to haul around so much stuff on my bike."

I laugh. "Your dad—Mr. Double Bass—told you that?"

"Funny, right? I didn't argue though. Keeping a low profile, you know. The last thing I need is my parents worrying every time I go out."

"I worry every time I go out." Getting to school this morning, I was a nervous wreck.

His eyes open wide. "Did something else happen? Did he—?"

"Nah. I just worry. I can't believe he attacked you like that. Sorry again."

"Meh," he says. "I survived."

We climb the stairs to William's place and knock on the door.

"Nikko! Chloë! How are you?" William holds my hand between his. I've barely talked to him lately, mostly because I don't know what to say. Do I tell him I miss my grandfather more than I thought possible, more even than my mom sometimes? I've gotten used to being far away from her. I can call her when I want to hear her voice. I don't think I'll ever get used to Uli not being across the street.

"I'm fine, thanks," I say. "How are you?"

"Oh, the usual aches and pains," William says.

"Sore knees, sensitive stomach. Don't ever get old. But enough of the organ recital. Do come in."

I smile, and we follow him down the narrow hallway to the living room. His apartment smells a little like mothballs, but there's something else too. Oranges, maybe. "Would you care for some tea? Kettle's just boiled." Without waiting for an answer, he disappears into the kitchen.

Nikko and I sit on a big, brown, flowery sofa. I wonder if William picked it out himself many years ago, or if he had a wife who did. Maybe losing a wife was one of the things he and my grandfather had in common.

"I'm ever so glad you came by," William says, carrying a tray with two mugs and a fancy teacup with a matching saucer. He places the teacup, brimming with milky tea, in front of me. "This cup was your grandfather's. Your father brought it to me a few days ago. It's a lovely memento."

I try to picture the delicate teacup in Uli's big, rough hands. I can't. "Was it my grandmother's?"

William shakes his head. "No, I bought it for your grandfather ages ago, as a joke. He always drank tea from old, chipped mugs as if he couldn't spare a dime, even when he had pots of money. I knew he'd never use a teacup, even if he had one— Uli was Uli, and that was one of the things I loved about him—but he always used the teacup to serve me tea. He said it suited my refined British manners better than his rustic German ones."

I can totally picture him saying that. But when did Uli ever have "pots of money"? He sure didn't by the time he died. Dad has met with the lawyer about the will. He says Uli must have been barely scraping by the last few years. What's left will just cover the cremation and lawyer fees. The house wasn't Uli's, and the contents weren't worth anything. "I didn't know he once had a lot of money."

"He did. Your father could tell you."

William and I look at each other like we both know that's not going to happen, so I change the subject. "I've been looking for Uli's seed collection. Do you know where it is?"

"Now that is a fine question, young lady," he says. "I must confess I never did share Uli's passion for vegetables."

"But didn't you help him write down the story of each seed?" I ask.

He nods. "Yes, but my interest went no further. I've always preferred a can of beans with toast to vegetables of any kind."

Oh.

"Chloë has a plan," Nikko says.

I do? I thought this was it—come here, talk to William, and go home with the seed collection. That was my only realistic plan.

"She wants to ask Uli's landlord if she can keep gardening long enough to harvest the seeds." Nikko tells William what Dad said about the landlord wanting to renovate before renting the house out again. Now that I hear my plan coming out of someone else's mouth, it sounds ridiculous.

William must think so too, because he whistles. "Well, you could ask Victor, I suppose. No harm in asking."

"Victor? That's the landlord's name?"

"Why, yes. Perhaps you haven't met him yet. He's not often home. He must be doing well for himself, though, if the fancy car outside his house is any sign."

I look at Nikko to see if he has any idea who William's talking about. He shakes his head.

"Must be hard on the boy, his father being away so much. I often see him sitting there on the steps—I think he's about your age—all alone."

Uh-oh. "You mean at the house across the street?"

"Yes, the gray one with the brown door. Next to your grandfather's. Victor moved in with his young wife and son not long before you arrived. It must be about a year ago now."

That old guy who told Slater to heat up the lasagna is his father? And Uli's landlord? I squeeze my eyes shut. No way am I going to knock on Slater's door to ask his family for a favor. Dad was right. It's a lost cause. Somehow I make it through the rest of our visit. As soon as we're in the stairwell, Nikko turns to me. "So do you want me to come with you when you talk to Victor?"

"You're kidding, right?" I ask.

"No."

"Seriously? Slater attacked you in the street yesterday for no good reason, and now we're going to show up at his house?"

Nikko shrugs. "I can be on the sidewalk with your cell phone, ready to call 9-1-1, if you'd rather go alone."

"Har, har."

He looks at me, apparently still waiting for me to answer his question.

I shake my head. "It's only a bunch of plants, right? I mean, Uli's gone. He never told me, or William, or my father, where he stashed the seed collection. It's not my fault he didn't make any plans for the future."

"You're talking yourself out of saving the garden." Nikko opens the door to his floor.

"I'm listening to my father."

"You're letting Slater win."

"I'm not letting Slater win. I'm protecting myself!"

Estelle's door flies open. "Whatever you're doing out there, could you please be quiet about it? Shouting in the hallways is not permitted."

I scowl at her and head downstairs, but Nikko follows me right to my apartment door and stands there, waiting.

"What?" I ask.

"You have to go see Victor," he says. "You'll never forgive yourself otherwise."

I cross my arms. He's right, and we both know it. "But Slater already thinks—"

"You're going to let the opinions of that idiot stop you from saving your grandfather's museum?" he asks.

"He's a big, strong, scary idiot."

Nikko grins and flexes his biceps. "Don't worry, you've got reinforcements."

"Wow, that makes me feel way better." But I can't help smiling.

"So you'll do it? You'll go talk to Victor?"

"I guess I might as well," I say. "I kind of feel like I'll never hear the end of it if I don't."

Nikko punches a fist in the air. "That's the spirit! Go get 'em."

What have I gotten myself into?

ELEVEN

"Sure you don't want to come out kayaking?" Dad asks for the millionth time. He's sitting on the couch with that box of cords, practicing knots. Every few minutes, he shows me a new one. "This one's a fireman's chair, for rescues. See, they slide the body through these loops, and they can lift a three-hundred-pound man this way, no problem." Then he undoes the whole thing, tries another knot and asks me about kayaking again. What happened to my homebody Montreal father?

"You go ahead, Dad," I say. "I've got a book report to finish."

But even when he's gone, I can't concentrate. I keep thinking about Uli. This afternoon would have been perfect for gardening—not too cool, not too warm. I call Sofia, but she doesn't answer. I wander into the kitchen and open the fridge, then close it again. In the end, with my book report only half done and the sun already going down, I put on my shoes and head across the street.

Technically, I'm not trespassing, because Uli's rent is paid until tomorrow, but I know Dad wouldn't want me here. I relax once I'm through the garden gate. The hedges are high, blocking even the windows of Slater's house, and I've got enough light left to see the paths between the beds. I wander along them, pulling out a sprig of bitter cress here and a creeping buttercup there. Sure, I can name all the weeds, but I still don't know if I'll be able to save the plants Uli cared so much about. Tomorrow I'll talk to Victor, but I have a feeling it won't do any good.

"Chloë! Are you in there?" Nikko is pounding on our door.

I open up, breakfast smoothie in my hand. "Where else would I be at this hour?"

"Have you seen the fence?"

"What fence?"

"The one that went up around Uli's place."

"What?"

"It must have gone up early this morning." He tells me about the huge No Trespassing sign and the big official notice saying that the entire block is up for redevelopment.

"The entire block?"

"Victor owns it all," Nikko says, "the houses, the grocery store, everything. I checked. City Hall has a whole list online of who wants to develop what. And this street isn't the only place where he's got property either. His company—it's called MacIntyre Holdings—owns land all over the city."

My head hurts. None of this makes any sense. Victor owns the grocery store. Uli and Dad both hate that store…because of Victor? If they hate him so much, then why did Uli keep renting the house from the guy? Why not move to a different neighborhood altogether?

"I thought you'd want to know," Nikko says.

I shake my head. "So much for asking Victor about working in the garden. If he's paranoid enough to put a fence around the whole property, he's never going to—"

"Not the whole property," Nikko says. "Just the front. You could still get his permission and then go in through the hole in the hedge. I read up about development permits. It takes months to get one. It looks like no one will be doing anything with the land in the meantime, so why wouldn't Victor let you look after the plants until they go to seed, right?"

Something tells me it's not going to be that easy.

I wait until Thursday, when Slater has soccer practice after school. Victor's silver BMW is parked in front of the house. I take a deep breath and climb the steps.

I knock. Nothing. I knock again, louder. The door flies open so fast that I jump backward. Victor doesn't look happy to see me. His obviously dyed black hair is greased back like Elvis Presley's. He squints at me through thick-framed glasses. "Can I help you?"

"I'm Chloë. My grandfather used to live next door." I'm sure he knows that. We've lived across the street from each other for months now, but he doesn't nod or anything, just stands there waiting for me to explain why I'm on his front steps. "I used to help Uli with the garden. I wanted to ask about the plan for—"

"You've read the signs?"

"Yes, and I—"

"Well, that's my plan. Now if you'll excuse me." He steps back into his house and closes the door in my face.

I stand there staring at the door for a few seconds. I turn to go down the steps, but then I see the chain-link fence. With my great-grandmother's apple tree behind it. My family's tree. My apples. I turn around and bang on the door again.

Victor glares at me. I talk fast, trying to say as much as possible before the door slams again. "It'll be a few months before you get permission to develop the land, right? So I thought I could keep working on Uli's garden until it goes to seed. I want to plant those seeds somewhere else next year because they're rare, and—"

"I don't care if they're the last seeds on Earth," he snaps. "I know how this works. Your grandfather kept a toehold by living there. Now that he's gone, you want to keep a toehold by gardening there. But the law is on my side. I bought the land fair and square. I've got the papers to prove it." He points to the fence and the large No Trespassing sign. "I intend to enforce that to the fullest extent of the law."

The door slams in my face again. I blink at it. Toehold? The law on his side? All I asked for was the plants, not the soil beneath them. What is Victor talking about?

"How was your day?" Dad carries two water glasses to the table, but along the way he glances back at his laptop on the kitchen counter and bumps into a chair. Water splashes onto the floor. Dad swears as if it's a really big deal.

I frown, not sure what he's so worked up about. If he knew about my chat with Victor this afternoon, I'd have found out already.

"Your mother's supposed to call around now," Dad says. "We have a supper date, the three of us."

"Oh?" I don't know what to make of that. My parents have been talking on the phone more since Mom was here. Dad goes into his room and closes the door whenever she calls. I've been thinking it's a good sign, but Dad's too jumpy tonight for this dinner date to mean anything good.

I bite into my burger, Dad sits down with his, and an awkward silence stretches between us. The laptop rings, and Dad lunges for it. He places Mom in the center of the table.

"Hi there. Bon appétit!" It's almost ten in Montreal, but she's sitting on our couch with a bowl of stir-fry that she shows off to the camera. For a moment, I'm impressed—Mom cooked!—but then she says, "Mongolian hot pot. A new place opened up where Película used to be."

"I know." I sound annoyed, even to myself. Annoyed that our neighborhood is changing without me. Annoyed that Mom and Dad have something big to announce, yet here we are, talking about Mongolian food.

My parents look at each other. Dad sets down his burger and clears his throat. "Chloë, there's something we need to tell you."

I hold my breath.

"We've decided to sell the house."

I look at him, and then at my mom, who starts blinking really fast. "I'm sorry, Chloë. I know this is hard for you, but your father and I have to face facts. We just—"

"What facts?" I ask. "We'll be there next month. We don't even have to come back here after that, right, Dad? We don't need to sell Uli's house because it belongs to someone else, and Dad won't need his job here anymore now that Uli's—"

"Chloë." Dad puts a hand on my arm. "Your mother and I have been talking a lot lately. We both need different things in our lives right now. Your mom wants to stay in Montreal, and I want to stay here. I'm not a big-city person. I never belonged there. I see that now."

"But what about me?" My vision goes blurry, but I will the tears away. "Where am I supposed to live? Saskatchewan? Halfway between the two of you?"

"That's what we want to talk about," Dad says. "You've got choices."

"What do you mean, I've got choices?" I'm shouting now, and my face is wet. "You two decide to sell our house and live on opposite sides of the country, and you call that a choice?"

"You'll have a home with either of us," Dad says. "Both of us. I'll be right here. Your mother wants to move to a condo closer to campus."

"It's lovely, Chloë." Her voice is soft, like she's coaxing a kitten out from behind a sofa. "Just a few steps from great bookstores and a block from the metro station."

"You already bought a place?" I croak.

"I put in an offer. I find out for sure next week."

I'm up and out the door before I even realize what's happening. I can hear Mom calling me back as I run down the hall and push through the back door. I take off across the parking lot and down the street. My only destination is Not Here, and I run flat out until breathing feels like knives between my ribs. Somewhere past the elementary school, I wish I'd brought my phone. It's next to the dinner table, recharging so I could finally arrange a time to talk to Sofia.

Sofia who tried to warn me. The night before we left Montreal, she was crying, saying I might never come back. I said I'd hitchhike home if I had to, but I meant it in the same way I'd promise to cut off my arm if it would save her from being abducted by aliens. I never imagined having to choose one place over the other.

Or hesitating about the choice.

But that was back when Montreal included a house where I lived with my parents, right next door to my best friend. That Montreal doesn't exist anymore and will never exist again. The closest I'll get is a bedroom in a condo that I share with my mother in a neighborhood I don't know. Sofia will be a forty-minute walk away. Dad will be on the other side of the country. That's not my idea of home. But a small apartment thousands of miles from where I grew up isn't home either. Home doesn't exist anymore.

I wander along the beach and through the park until dark. Then, without really thinking about it, I head back to our street. I stop next to Uli's hedge and find the spot where a big, frilly cedar branch blocks a clearing behind.

I push the frond aside, just to test it. I have no intention of going in, of course. Victor's words—*to the fullest extent of the law*—are booming through my thoughts. From here I can see the chain link and its No Trespassing signs gleaming in the moonlight. I'd be an idiot to break into the garden. The same way Uli was an idiot to plant everything—even his mother's apple tree—on land that didn't belong to him, as if home could be carried with you like seeds in your boot. As if gardening on a patch of unfamiliar earth could bring back everything that had been taken away.

I push the branch aside, look both ways and squeeze through. Until I find that seed collection, I need to keep these plants alive. I'm not letting go of this garden until I can take what's mine.

TWELVE

Maybe Uli thought the end of the world was coming. That would explain the stockpiles in his basement and the two giant rain barrels next to the house. Whatever he was thinking, the rainwater and his plastic-bottle irrigation system mean I can still save the heirlooms.

I push open the greenhouse doors, letting out a rush of hot air into the cool darkness. The tomato plants are growing fast. So is the corn. In just a few weeks, the little stalks have grown as tall as my hand.

The watering bucket is right by the door where I left it. On the way to the rain barrel, I spot the lettuce—an entire row of blue-green leaves, ready to eat. Uli showed me how to pick the outside leaves so that the middle of the plant keeps growing and goes to seed. I've been doing that, eating as I garden. I also took lots of peas and favas to Nikko because Dad wouldn't want me bringing them home. But soon this garden will produce way more than Nikko's family and I can eat.

As I fill each plastic water bottle, I think of Uli growing up in bombed-out cities, eating whatever he and his mom could scrounge. He would have hated food going to waste in his own garden.

That's when I remember the soup kitchen. I smile as I hurry around with my bucket. The last thirsty bed is the spinach. Watering done, I find some plant pots and dig out a few of the big Scottish blue kale. I read online that kale doesn't mind being transplanted. I hope that's true, because I want to plant these in a place where I can look after them. I grab four potted tomato plants and the corn. Then I fill a bucket with ripe produce and push all of it out through the hedge onto the sidewalk, like an eat-your-veggies version of Robin Hood. I wish I could bring more, but I have to be realistic.

It'll be all I can do to ferry this load across the street without being spotted.

Nikko answers the door as soon as I knock. It's late, but I saw from the street that his lights were still on.

"What happened to you?" he asks. I've stashed the plants and the veggie harvest in Dad's tool shed. I don't know exactly what I'm going to do with them, but they're safe for tonight. And I did the whole transfer without a soul finding out. I think. No one saw me from the street. No one was watching through the building windows, not even the cat. I met Estelle on the way in, but maybe she thought I was coming back from a walk.

Nikko frowns. "You've got dirt on your cheek and…cedar bits in your hair?" His eyes widen. He calls back into his apartment to say he's going out. Then he lowers his voice. "Follow me."

We hurry down the hall, past Estelle's door, into the stairwell and up to the top floor. He points to the metal ladder that leads to the roof. "We can talk up there."

I've been on a few rooftops in Montreal, wind-swept gardens above twenty-story buildings with a view from Mount Royal to the St. Lawrence. I've never been up here though. It never seemed worth the bother. What can you see from a little four-story building?

As my head pokes through the hatch, I look into a sea of stars. By the time I'm standing on the shingles, I feel like I'm in a wraparound movie theater, watching a documentary about constellations. Except this is real. And I'm here.

Nikko tiptoes to the far end. I follow. We sit in the darkness with the open hatch casting up a cozy glow. "The good thing about living in a building full of seniors," he says, "is that no one ever uses the stairs anymore, never mind the ladder to the roof. No one knows we're here."

I decide right now that I'm not going to tell Sofia about this. She'll turn it into a romantic adventure and will never believe me when I say I don't feel romantic about Nikko at all. "I got into the garden," I whisper.

He laughs. "Yeah. No kidding. The cedar in your hair gave it away."

His fingers are warm and light on my scalp as he tries to get the tree bits out. (Definitely not telling Sofia about that either.) I tell him everything that's happened today, from the conversation with Victor to my parents selling our house to me stealing plants. He listens and frowns in all the right places, but he's silent until I say, "I got some produce for you to bring to the soup kitchen too."

"Perfect. What have you got? And what does it taste like?"

"It's blue lettuce, and it tastes like…well… lettuce. If I had the seed collection, I'd be able to tell you exactly where it came from."

"Uli would be glad you didn't let it go to waste," Nikko says.

I've already told him we've got kale, corn and tomato plants in the shed. "But most of the plants, like the lettuce, can't be transplanted once they're in the ground. I'll have to wait for them to go to seed."

"But that'll take months!" he says. "How will you get in to do the watering with Slater living next door and Estelle-the-Eye living across the street?"

It does sound crazy when he puts it that way. "Slater can't see over the hedge from his house," I offer. It's the best I've got.

"But anyone on the street can see you breaking in." He leans back on his hands and stretches out his long legs. "What if we could save the plants in a legal way? Involve the local media or get people in the neighborhood to sign a petition? Victor owns the local grocery store. He won't want the whole neighborhood against him."

"How do you come up with this stuff?"

"My parents are always writing letters," he says. "To the newspaper, the mayor, the provincial government, you name it."

I think about that for a moment, but it's not going to work. "Uli said he refilled the water bottles every day in the summer, and it's hot already. The plants could die while we're gathering signatures."

"Oh yeah. I guess that's true," he says. "But you know you're going to get caught, right?"

I nod, even though I don't want to. This was the moment where he was supposed to say, *I'll help you with the watering every few days, and after you're gone, I'll take over, watering, harvesting—*

Who am I kidding? This whole thing is nuts, but it's the only plan I've got so far. I have to go with it, because if the plants die now, it won't matter how many amazing plans I come up with later on.

"I'll help you plant the stuff you've already rescued," Nikko says, "if you want."

It's a start.

THIRTEEN

I smooth my hair. Nikko assured me that I didn't have a speck of plant life in it anymore, but I feel like Dad'll take one look at me and know where I've been. I take a deep breath and push open our apartment door.

Dad jumps up from the couch, his knotting cords falling to the floor. "Thank goodness."

He doesn't need to say he's been worried. I can see it on his face. I feel a twinge of guilt for being out so long after dark. "Sorry, I—"

"I know. You needed to get out. To think. Are you—?" He hesitates. "Are you feeling better?"

I'm not furious anymore, like I was when I flew out of here. Mostly because I refuse to think about my parents splitting up. I'm focusing on the garden now. "Yes, I'm better."

"I'll text your mom and let her know you're home."

This is how it's going to be from now on, I realize. I'll be living either with Dad or Mom, and they'll text each other about what I'm up to. My eyes feel hot, and Dad comes over to hug me. "I'm sorry, Chloë. I know this is hard for you."

No kidding. I bite back the words and rest my head against his shoulder. When he lets go, I kick off my shoes. One of them hits a cardboard box on the floor. "What's that?"

"A few of Uli's things that I set aside for William. He looked through and took what he wanted but left the rest for us."

I open the box. Albums. A whole stack of photo albums. I crouch down to open the first, and there's my grandmother, smiling, under the apple tree, with my child-dad up in the branches. "You didn't want the photos?"

"Please don't open those now," Dad says. "You can look at them later. Right now I need to talk to you about the house. Our house. In Montreal."

I step away from the box and flop down on the couch, but I'm not giving up. Not this time. "Why did you hate him so much?"

"I didn't." Dad picks up a cord again and begins another knot. "We had a troubled relationship. It's not the same."

I wait for him to continue, but he doesn't.

"Will you ever tell me?" I ask. "Because I still don't get it. Why did we move across the country to be here when you could barely stand to be in the same room? Why are you staying now that he's gone? None of it makes sense."

He's got tears in his eyes when he turns to me. "I came back for a lot of reasons, Chloë, and I brought you with me for a lot of reasons too. But the main one is I love you, and I couldn't stand the idea of not seeing you every day."

"But Mom—" My voice is barely a whisper. I don't know what I'm trying to ask. If Mom wouldn't miss me as much maybe? How did they decide this?

"She misses you terribly, but she wanted you to get to know your grandfather. That was always important to her. She said you needed to know where you came from, even if you didn't want to stay."

I think about that for a moment. "Did you know then that you'd stay?" *Please say no. Please say that you weren't lying about that when we came here.*

"I didn't have a clue," Dad says. "I knew I wanted you to have time to be a kid without two parents fighting every night. I wanted to give you a chance to throw rocks into the ocean. Go for bike rides. Live a simpler life for a while. I didn't plan to stay for very long. But then William found me this job, and—"

"William?"

"He mentioned it to my father, who mentioned it to me. Everything was set into motion after that, and here we are." He waves a hand at our furniture and the wall he transformed to lively orange.

It takes me a while to process this. "I didn't know Mom cared about Uli so much."

"She didn't know him well," he says. "They only met a few times, but family is family. She cares about us, so she cared about him."

Kind of like how I care about my great-grand-mother because Uli cared about her. Enough to plant that tree and tell me about her years and years after she died.

"I wish Mom lived here." I know it's stupid, but I can't help it. How do I choose between my parents and between two completely different lives?

Dad smiles. "Can you imagine your mom living in Victoria?"

I can't. Mom's a big-city person. She loves her university, meeting friends after work for a glass of wine, finding vintage clothing at the fripperies and going to concerts. Some weekends, we'd drag her up Mount Royal for a walk in the woods, but she went because Dad and I wanted to. It's not something she'd ever have done on her own.

"I loved Montreal when I first got there too," Dad says. "But I missed the ocean—and the trees, and the lakes, and hiking. I left Victoria to get away from my father, but this place never stopped feeling like home. I wanted to come back."

"Even if your father was still here."

"Even if, and because. I wanted to put some things to rest with him," he says. "You're right. I owe you an explanation. I'll give you one soon,

I promise, but I need to figure out how to tell the story respectfully, in a way that doesn't sound like I'm judging him. He was a good man. He just took too many risks. I guess he didn't know how to be any other way."

I don't say anything. One wrong word, and my dad might change his mind. He's never promised to tell me soon about what happened between him and his father. I don't want to push it. Luckily, we have no shortage of huge, life-altering events to talk about, so I change the subject. "You told Mom you wanted to move back to Victoria, and she thought it was a good idea?"

He shrugs. "We weren't getting along. I'd lost my job. My father had just had a stroke. Coming here felt like the best thing to do at the time." He watches my face for a moment. "Neither one of us wanted to hurt you, Chloë. I hope you know that."

I nod. That, at least, I've known all along.

FOURTEEN

I don't recognize the grocery store right away. The photo is black and white, the parking lot is edged with flowers, and the painted wooden sign says *Gwen's General Store*. Not Smith's. Two people stand in front of the store, a tall man with a bushy beard, and a boy a little younger than me with thick glasses and shaggy hair. My dad. Uli is beaming and has his arm around Dad's shoulders. Dad looks uncomfortable, like he feels the way I do about photo ops.

Uli Becher's popular local store provided Thanksgiving dinner for 180 people at the St. John's soup kitchen this past weekend, the caption says.

I frown. Uli's store?

It was late. Dad had already gone to bed, but I'd known I wouldn't be able to sleep until I'd looked through the photo albums. So I'd brought William's cardboard box into my bedroom and closed the door. Most of the albums were labeled by year (*Our Family 1977–1983*) but some had specific titles. I turned the pages and saw Dad as a chubby baby, a serious toddler and a smiling boy. His mom was almost always with him. I guess Uli was behind the camera. Below each photo was a small white tag with the date and usually the place, written in a graceful handwriting. The last date was in 1988, the year before my grandmother died.

Garden began the year after she died and had fewer photos—one of Uli's yard, all lawn like at Victor's place; my father at about twelve, crouched down among seedlings; both him and Uli with an enormous pumpkin. It must be the one that Dad talked about at the memorial. I set the photo aside to show to him later. After that the photos were more random. None of them were labeled with dates.

I hadn't known what to expect from *Sailing*. The first pictures were close-ups of docked boats and dotted horizons, all labeled with dates in the early 1970s. A few pages later, the photos were from the mid-eighties. Every one was of my grandmother, steering, raising masts or relaxing on the deck in the sunshine. Most were badly composed and out of focus, but near the end of the book, they got better. She was paler and thinner though.

At the bottom of the box was a stack of photos and newspaper clippings held together with an elastic band. I flipped through. Vegetable pictures, an apartment building I didn't recognize and the clipping about the grocery store.

"Dad?" I'm out in the hallway and knocking on his door. I don't care that it's late and I should be asleep and that he probably already is. A few hours ago I was fine waiting until Dad was ready to tell this story, but now I have too many questions. I'll never fall asleep with all of them flying around in my head. "Dad, wake up."

I hear a loud snort from behind his door. "Huh? What? Chloë?" He opens the door, blinking in the hallway's brightness.

I hold up the newspaper article. "Uli owned the store?"

He passes a hand over his face. "Chloë. It's the middle of the night."

"But I don't understand. How did Uli go from owning the store to not setting foot anywhere near it?"

He squints at me for a few more seconds. "Okay, I need a coffee. Let me at least get a coffee first."

I sit in the living room and wait. When he sits down with his steaming mug, he takes a deep breath. "You know part of the story already. Your grandfather grew up very poor. He came to Canada an orphan, his uncle was an alcoholic, and his aunt was crazy, so after a few years, he took off and hitchhiked west."

I tuck my knees under my chin. "Yup, Uli told me that part."

"By then, he spoke English well, but he didn't have any skills that could earn him money—nothing except what he'd learned on the farm with his uncle. He got a job with a landscaping company and started gardening. He also started gambling. And he was lucky at first. By the time he was twenty-one, he had saved enough to buy a house. He learned about investing. He knew how to stretch a dollar."

He always drank tea from old, chipped mugs as if he couldn't spare a dime, even when he had pots of money, William had said. I guess when you grow up with nothing, saving every penny becomes a habit. But then why gamble? It doesn't make sense. "At some point he bought the grocery store too?"

Dad nods. "Eventually he owned a lot of things—that store and all three houses across the street."

"The entire block?" Just like Victor.

Another nod. He knocks back the rest of his coffee. "He got the first house and the grocery store before he married Mom. Then he stopped gambling. He didn't start again until she got sick."

"What?" I ask. "She was dying of cancer, and he went out gambling?"

He lets out a long, slow breath. "It's an addiction, Chloë. Addictions are hardest to resist when we're scared and trying to cope. When Mom got sick, he was terrified, and he did what he'd always done when he was scared. He played poker. She died, and then he gambled even more."

"Until he lost it all." It's weird to know the beginning and the end of the story before hearing the middle.

"First he lost the grocery store. He wagered it. In a poker game."

No way.

"He was drunk that night, and he wanted to win an apartment building. For me."

This is making less sense all the time.

"He knew I wanted to sail around the world, and he figured that if I owned an apartment building and everyone in it was paying me rent, then I wouldn't ever have to worry about money again. He was trying to help me live my dream. I see that now, but I didn't see it then because that poker game is when he lost the store. Without that income, he had to start selling off other stuff. Like my sailboat."

What? "You had your own sailboat? How old were you?" I can't believe I never knew these things about him.

"It was my mother's first, but Dad hated being out on the water. So after she died, he gave it to me. Mom had been taking me out sailing since I was a few months old. We were going to sail down to Mexico someday, but then she got sick." He looks down at his hands.

I feel like everything I thought I knew about my grandfather—and my father too—is shifting. Like the kaleidoscope I had when I was three. I used to love looking inside, twisting the end and watching the bright little pieces shift to form new shapes. But I hate this changing image of Uli. How do I match my gentle gardener grandfather with this drunken gambler who risked everything? I guess that's why Dad never wanted to tell me this story. Would I have wanted to spend time with Uli if I'd known what he was like before?

"Dad hired someone to look after the boat. He paid for sailing lessons too, and it wasn't the same as being out on the water with Mom, but I still felt close to her out there. Everything—her death, Dad's gambling—was easier to handle when I was sailing.

I told Dad I was going to Mexico someday, just like Mom and I had planned to, and I started saving every cent. I even started racing. There was serious money in that."

"But then he sold the boat."

"Exactly." Dad pushes up from the sofa and takes his mug back to the kitchen.

"Wait," I say. "How did Victor wind up with everything?"

"He won the store. Then Uli lost a few bets with other people. Victor offered to buy one of his houses. After that, each time Dad had cash-flow problems, he went to Victor. One day, when he had to sell his own house to make ends meet, Victor bought it but agreed to let Dad stay there as a tenant until he died."

I know how this works, Victor had said. *Your grandfather kept a toehold by living there. Now that he's gone, you want to keep a toehold by gardening there. But the law is on my side. I bought the land fair and square.* It makes sense now. "But at some point he stopped gambling, right? I mean—"

"Yes," Dad says. "He went to some program or something. It worked, but by then he had lost everything. He never had much money again after that."

"Did you ever talk about it with him?" I can guess the answer, but I still want to hear what he says.

"I think he wanted to," Dad says. "He sent me a pamphlet about the addiction program he went through. It said that part of the healing process was to talk with family about the problems that the addiction had caused in everyone's life. I think that's why he came to see us in Montreal. He probably saved for ages to afford that trip. But I didn't want to talk. It felt like too little, too late. I still remember the look on his face when we said goodbye at the airport that time. Like he was a little boy trying not to cry."

And now Dad's crying. He sits down on the sofa with his head in his hands. I put an arm around him. "He knew you loved him," I say. "You came here when he needed you, didn't you?"

"I hope he knew," Dad whispers. "I really hope so."

"I'm sure of it."

"I'm sorry, Chloë," he says. "I wish things had been different."

Back in my bedroom, I pin the newspaper clipping to my wall. It's a picture of a man who would eventually sell his son's sailboat, but it's also a picture of a man and a boy who planted a garden—a garden that I'm going to save.

FIFTEEN

"You look ready for anything."

Nikko is standing in our parking lot, wearing long sleeves, gardening gloves, long pants, socks and boots, despite the June heat. I can smell the citronella from here.

"You look like you're ready to go hiking in the Amazon," I say. "How did you explain your outfit to your parents?"

"The same way I explained to Estelle why I was poking around in the tool shed." He lowers his voice dramatically. "Scientific experiment."

We climb onto our bikes. His is hitched up to his dad's bike trailer, but instead of pulling a double bass, he's got a trailer full of plants. "Onward!"

A few minutes later, we're flying down Vancouver Street to Beacon Hill Park. When Nikko first suggested it as a new home for some of Uli's plants, I thought he was nuts. As much as I'm tempted to plant kale in the middle of the putting green, or a tomato plant on the cricket pitch, or squash between the rosebushes, none of them would last more than a couple of hours before some paid caretaker ripped it out. But Nikko said he knew a good spot.

Nikko and I pedal toward the ocean, veering left to a tiny forested patch that I've never paid much attention to. Nikko says it's the only area that's still wild-ish, and you're more likely to see a barred owl in here than a parks employee. So chances are, no one'll spot our plantings. That's our theory anyway.

We stop on one of the trails and lock our bikes. I grab the pots of kale, remembering how Uli said these bluish-green leaves are fantastic with sausages. Or as kale chips. (Ugh. That still sounds horrible, but I'm determined to at least try it once, in Uli's honor. Nikko says his parents have a recipe. Apparently, the secret is massaging the leaves. Who thinks up these things?) Stepping over fallen logs and roots, we tiptoe between the trees until we're far enough into the woods that no one will see us from the path.

"What if they reseed themselves and this spot becomes a local legend?" Nikko puts on a deep documentary-narrator voice. "Every summer, families from all over the city set off into the woods in search of feral kale."

I laugh. Sofia would too. Kale-hunting parties. You can't get more west coast than that.

"Let's hope the deer don't get it first."

"Deer?" I ask.

"From Government House. They have a big patch of land to roam on there, but they always get out and eat people's gardens too. I hope they like kale about as much as you like asparagus."

I groan, but there's nothing to do but keep planting. Once every kale plant is in the ground, we head back to the trailer. Nikko consults his list of destinations. "Next stop, Fernwood. I found an empty lot that's begging for corn. The subdivision permit will take months to go through. Plenty of time for a harvest."

"Let me guess," I say. "You looked it up online?"

"No, someone from the homeschooling network told me."

I frown. "How did that topic come up?"

"I've been getting the word out about our little garden project," he says. "My homeschooling friends are all over the idea. They even offered to help."

"What?" I drop my voice to a whisper. "You've told the homeschooling network about this? Are you completely nuts?"

"Don't worry, Chloë. No one's going to find out that—"

"Are you kidding?" My voice is too loud now, but I can't help it. "Victoria is the size of an anthill. The school bully is the son of my grandfather's enemy. My teacher's wife is my dad's barber. Someone farts and it's on the evening news. Of course they're going to find out who's stealing the plants and relocating them!"

"Chill, Chloë," Nikko says. "I didn't say *Please join Chloë Becher as she illegally enters the property of one of Victoria's richest and most bitter landlords.* I told them about an empty lot I always pass on my way home from the soup kitchen. I said I wished the city made landowners plant gardens until they started building. We'd have way more fresh food that way."

"Oh." My heart slows to a normal pace.

"One of my buddies lives across from an empty lot—the one in Fernwood—and he said he'd help work on a garden there. A bunch of other people said the same thing. That's all."

"This is crazy," I say. "The kale is going to be deer food. The landowner's going to rip out the corn. I've got a garden full of plants that I need to water every few days, and Victor—"

"We're doing our best," Nikko says. "Uli would be grateful."

I keep pedaling and try to believe he's right.

"So what's the deal?" Sofia says. "Are you moving back here or what?"

I've told her everything, from Slater attacking Nikko to guerilla gardening in Fernwood. She was quiet almost the whole time, a rare thing for Sofia. Now I'm silent too, because she's just asked a question I've been thinking about for days now. Every time I imagine moving back to Montreal to live with Mom in a condo in an unfamiliar neighborhood, I feel sad. Sure, it would be great to see Sofia again, but we'd still live too far apart for things to be the way they were. I don't know how I'm going to tell Sofia this though.

"I'm going to miss you," she says.

"But nothing's decided yet, and I—"

"I'm going to miss you," she says again, "but you can't get rid of me by moving to the other side of the country, you know. I'm coming to visit. I've already looked up flights. I can come in the first week of August. I want to meet Nikko and see your garden and dip my foot in the ocean and watch you actually riding a bike."

I don't protest this time. If I moved in with Mom, I'd be saying goodbye to all that stuff to live in a tiny condo in a neighborhood where I know no one. "I think you'll like it here," I say instead.

I need to find another way in to Uli's garden. Every time I walk past the hedge, I can see the hole I squeeze through. I'm sure everyone else can see it too. The branches aren't straightening to cover it up the way they used to. But maybe I'm just being paranoid. Most people aren't looking for secret passageways when they walk past a hedge. The same way they're not looking for fruit on the cherry blossom trees. I look up at the tree on the boulevard. The flowers are long gone—it's all green leaves now—but at the ends of the lower branches are small green fruits that make me smile. In a few more weeks, the cherries will be ripe. I can't wait to taste Uli's public art.

The moon isn't as bright as it was two nights ago, but I have Dad's headlamp with me this time. I'm trying to water without a sound. I know exactly where my feet must fall on the path to avoid tripping. I'm extra careful by the concrete pad under the rain barrels, worried I'll trip or knock a lid off by mistake. I'm jumpy tonight, hearing noises that don't make sense, like footfalls on the sidewalk outside, again and again, as if someone's out there pacing at two in the morning.

Focus. I grab the watering bucket to dip it in the rain barrel, but this barrel's almost empty. I have to tip the whole thing toward me to reach the water. For a moment I consider uncovering the full one, but I've never done that before. What if I fumble, and the cover goes crashing to the ground?

I lean farther into the almost-empty barrel. Half a bucket. It's as much as I can get. It'll have to do for now. I lower the tilted barrel back onto the ground, and that's when I hear it: a small clang, not coming from outside this time, but from right under the barrel. I train my headlamp onto the ground. The light falls on a little metal plate built into the concrete. I roll the barrel carefully to one side. In the middle of the plate is a small, circular hole. I could stick my finger in and lift it right out. My heart beats faster. Only one thing mattered enough to Uli for him to build a special hiding place for it.

I lift the plate and pull a large, red metal box from its secret spot. It doesn't weigh much, but then again, neither did the shoebox full of seeds that Uli showed me in his greenhouse all those months ago. It's the right size. It's also locked. I have no idea how I'm going to open it, but that hardly matters right now. I've got the seeds—I'm sure of it. Victor can set fire to the rest of this garden for all I care!

I hurry across the yard to the exit and freeze. Because someone's watching me through the hole in the hedge. It's a face I don't recognize, a man's face. I panic. Running will get me nowhere. Screaming will wake the neighbors—which would save me from a crazy who walks the streets at night but would also land me in a whole pile of trouble.

He pushes his way through the hedge into the garden. I can see now that he's wearing a uniform. Not the police. A security guard. "I saw you go in, young lady. The police will be here in a few minutes. I've already got pictures, so I wouldn't bother bolting, if I were you. You might as well give me the box." He holds out his hand. "You can't take it with you."

SIXTEEN

"The police convinced Victor not to press charges,"
Dad tells my mom. His voice is calm now, not
like when the police brought me home last night.
"Chloë's young and didn't mean any harm, so the
courts probably wouldn't bother with it anyway."

It's evening in Montreal, and Mom's still at the
office. She's sitting in her desk chair, this horrified
look on her face. "What were you thinking, Chloë?
I thought we raised you better than this!"

I stare at her. "This has nothing to do with how
you raised me! I wanted to—"

"I don't care what you wanted to do, Chloë! You
were trespassing! And stealing! There's never any
excuse for that."

"But—"

"I can't believe this." She squeezes her eyes shut. I don't think she's crying, but she looks wounded, which almost feels worse, like she can never trust me again. "Chloë, all this sneaking around may seem like fun to you, but—"

"You think I did this for fun?" My voice is too loud, but I don't care. I push myself up from the sofa. Dad grabs my arm, but I wrench my hand free and stomp off to my bedroom, the only place left for me to go.

Please pick up. Phoning to apologize.

I blink at Mom's text. It's breakfast time, almost noon in Montreal. But that's not why I'm surprised. Mom apologizing? Now there's a first. I turn the ringer back on. The next time it sounds, I pick up.

"I talked to your Dad," she says. "And to Sofia."

"I know. She texted me." She sent a photo of the For Sale sign in front of our house too.

"She told me more about Uli's garden," Mom says. "I didn't know you cared so much about the plants."

"Yeah, you made that pretty clear."

"I'm sorry," she says. "I'm sorry for a lot of things. You know I didn't set out for everything to happen this way, right?"

I don't answer. I'm looking through my tiny bedroom window to the bush planted in front of it. My bedroom at home looked onto our balcony and down to Sofia's backyard. I wonder what the bedroom in Mom's new condo is like, but I don't wonder enough to actually want to stay there.

It's Mom who finally breaks the silence. "Thanks for answering the phone. I'll talk to you soon. And hold on to that Sofia. She's a keeper."

Only Nikko bangs on our apartment door like that, not a crisp *rat-tat-tat* like Estelle, but a full-bodied *bam-bam-bam*, as if the door is in the way of sharing the best news on the planet.

"Nice shirt," I say. It's gray with a sprouting seed on the front. "Where'd you get it?"

"A friend made it. But I designed it. We made one for you too," he calls back over his shoulder because he's already halfway down the hall. "Can you come out the front? I have something to show you."

I follow him to the lobby and through the front door. Across the street a crowd has formed. They're shouting something I can't make out, but it's happy shouting. At least forty people are gathered in front of the chain-link fence. They've got cardboard signs saying things like *Seeds Are Our Future* and *Save Our Vegetables!* and even *Save the Bees!* Cars are slowing as they pass. Someone shows up with a TV camera.

"Who are all these guys?" I ask Nikko.

"People who don't want Victor to turf the seed collection," he says. "Gardeners, Quakers, soup-kitchen people, homeschooling friends. *Choose your battle*, Uli said. This seemed like a good one."

Without thinking, I hug him. He staggers back, his face turning red. Dad saves us the trouble of figuring out what to say next. He shows up behind me with two pieces of cardboard in hand. "Shall we join them, Chloë?"

"You have signs too?" I ask. "You knew about this?"

"Nikko might have mentioned it."

"But Victor—"

"We'll stand on this side of the street." Dad hands me a sign, and we cross the lawn to our corner. From there I can see that Slater is out on his lawn too, watching everyone and smiling. Okay, it's more of a smirk, and he's probably thinking we're all a bunch of losers, but he's not making anyone's life miserable at the moment, for a change.

The camera guy pans the crowd of protesters. A few minutes later a woman with glossy black hair and perfect makeup interviews Nikko and then me. I talk about kale that can grow as tall as me, the blue squashes Uli loved, white turnips that are pink inside, purple beans, and the people who gave Uli the seeds in the first place. "If my grandfather had had a dying wish," I say, "it would have been to save those seeds for future generations."

The woman smiles and puts the microphone away. "Thanks. That was great." She hands me her card. "By the way, have you heard about the seed library?"

"Seed library?" I ask.

"It launched last spring. I did a story on it, and I follow them now on Twitter." She explains how anyone with a public library card can borrow seeds to grow in their own gardens. When those plants go to seed, people harvest, dry and return the new seeds to the library for the next season. "They accept donations too. Someone left them a huge collection a few months ago, and people are all excited about it. It includes some really rare seeds, I guess."

Nikko scribbles in his notebook. "Any idea who the donor was?"

"No," she says. "I'm sure you could find out though."

"I'll do that." Nikko catches my eye, and I stifle a laugh because I know we don't need to try to find out who it was.

Now I know why I couldn't find the seed collection. Turns out, Uli did have a plan after all. All these weeks while I was watering, trespassing and guerilla gardening—becoming a much bolder person than I've ever been before—the library was preparing his collection for the whole city to use.

I made a promise to the people who gave me the seeds, Uli said. *Darned if I'll go back on it now.*

When Dad told Uli not to garden this year, my grandfather answered with his best poker face. He even managed to look a bit offended. But I see now that he was bluffing. He'd already looked after the future of the seed collection. What he didn't want to give up on was me. And our family. Asking me to garden with him was his last-ditch attempt to repair everything that had fallen apart since he'd planted the garden in the first place, the year my grandmother died.

Even though I'd thought he was a little bit crazy, I'd agreed to it, because I'd left my whole life in Montreal, and I had nothing to lose. I had no idea then that by digging in the dirt, I'd get the stories of my great-grandmother's tree and my grandmother's sailboat and why Dad had left this place and why he wanted to come back. But most of all, I'd get to know my grandfather.

"What do you think was in the red box then?" I ask Nikko when the reporter has gone back to her car.

"Who knows?" He moves his head in the direction of the crowd across the street. "Do you think we should tell them to stop protesting? That the lost collection has been found?"

"Nah," I say. "I bet Uli's enjoying watching this, wherever he is."

"Digging into his big bowl of chocolate ice cream in the sky."

SEVENTEEN

Slater's family moves out in August. I don't know where they go, but with any luck, it's to a fancy suburb far, far away. The house stays empty. The house next to it still has renters, but Estelle says they'll be leaving in October. Uli's place looks pretty much like it did when the fence went up. The thyme in the front yard is neat and tidy—nothing like regular grass would have been by now. If you look closely, you can see apples on his mother's tree, still green but getting bigger.

Our Montreal house sells in September. When we hear the news, Dad and I go for a walk on the beach. At first we talk about this and that:

my new classes, Mom's new condo and Dad's plan to buy his own kayak—less expensive than a sailboat and much easier to store. Behind Dad, an old man tosses a stick for his dog. Cyclists along the roadway shout to each other in a windswept conversation.

"We should check out some of Uli's seeds from the library," I say. I've been reading about it online. The library offers a short workshop where you learn how to harvest and dry the seeds. After that you have access to any of the seeds in the library. "I want to plant apple trees."

Dad shakes his head. "There wouldn't be apple seeds in the collection."

"Of course there would be! Uli's mom trekked across Europe with them in her boot, and he went back to Edmonton to—"

Again Dad shakes his head. "Apples are like people. Children never look exactly like their parents. When you grow apple trees from seed, the fruit on the new tree never turns out exactly like the fruit it came from."

I frown. "But then how—?"

"The apple Uli's mother brought from Poland was small and mealy. But when Uli planted the seeds in Edmonton, the apples that grew on one of those trees were big and sweet," Dad says. "He wanted apples like those ones, so he went back to the farm and cut off a few buds—scions, they're called. Little slivers of tree with buds on them. Then he grafted the scions onto rootstock."

I stare at my father. Grafting. Like what Uli did with the cherry trees. I didn't know Dad knew all this stuff. Or cared. But maybe all these years caring was just too painful, the same way it hurt for him to visit Uli's garden or go into his house. "Rootstock? What's rootstock?"

"It's part of a plant—the roots and a bit of the stump. You can choose different kinds, depending on how tall you want your tree to be. Then you graft parts of another plant onto that rootstock so it all grows together as a single tree."

"Huh." Why has no one—not even Uli—ever told me this before?

Dad's really getting into the conversation now. "The rootstock part grows down into the soil.

The grafted-on parts grow up and determine the kind of fruit. If you graft a few buds from Uli's apple tree onto some rootstock, it'll bear apples just like the ones on the tree you grafted from. They'll be clones, actually."

Weird. But excellent too. "I always pictured Uli bringing back seeds from Edmonton. I even imagined him tucking them into his shoe, like his mom had."

"Nope. Little branches. He grafted them and planted a tree at each of his houses."

I turn to look at him. "What do you mean, *at each of his houses*? Are you saying there are three of Uli's apple trees?"

"There were," Dad says. "The one behind the rental got cut down."

"But there's still one behind Victor's house?" Which is empty at the moment, as we happen to know.

Dad nods. "Yup. Same variety."

I turn and head toward the road.

"Where are you going?" He hurries to catch up with me.

"Where do we get rootstock? We have some grafting to do."

"Now?" he asks.

"No time like the present," I say. "How many buds do we need?"

"Depends how many trees you want to grow. I can ask if we can plant them around the building, or maybe we could plant a few in different places around the city." He winks. "We'd increase our odds that way."

"Gambling with fruit trees," I say. "Uli would have loved that."

ACKNOWLEDGMENTS

Uli's garden came together with the help of countless people, and the same goes for this book! Thank you to BC Arts Council for the funding that allowed me to work on this project. Thanks also to Doug Woodworth, Jerome Bender, James Craig and Matthew Rutherford for speaking with this random children's author who called up with questions about gambling and trespassing. Thank you, Susan Braley, Susannah Adams and Farheen Haq, for listening to me talk endlessly about this story and encouraging me to keep going. Robin Stevenson and Kari Jones, I appreciate your astute and honest feedback at particularly confusing stages of the manuscript. Bob McInnes, thanks for lending me your ice-cream-rescue story. (Bob once rescued ice cream in much the same fashion that Nikko did—a true bicycle visionary!)

Thank you, Chris Adams, for being so passionate about this book and for weeding out agricultural errors. (Pun intended. Sorry. I couldn't resist.) I'm grateful to everyone at Orca Book Publishers who helped bring this project into the world, especially my editor, Tanya Trafford, who has an incredible gift for seeing the potential in a story and who masterfully guided me in just the direction I needed to go, and Rachel Page for the beautiful book design. And thanks to Julie McLaughlin for the awesome cover that makes me grin every time I think about it. Finally, thank you, Gastón and Maia, my excellent family, who have cheered me along every step of the way. It really takes a village to write a book, and I've been incredibly lucky with mine. Thank you all.